SCHOOL

SCHOOL

A NOVEL
RAY LEVY

TUSCALOOSA

FC2 is an imprint of the University of Alabama Press

Inquiries about reproducing material from this work should be addressed to the University of Alabama Press

Book Design: Publications Unit, Department of English, Illinois State
    University; Director: Steve Halle, Production Assistant: Maggie Wolff
Cover design: Lou Robinson
Typeface: Adobe Jenson Pro

Library of Congress Cataloging-in-Publication Data is available from the Library of Congress.
ISBN: 978-1-57366-202-4
E-ISBN: 978-1-57366-904-7

CONTENTS

I. DIALOGUE BETWEEN A PRIEST AND A DYING MAN

When you write about yourself, I've noticed, you place the terms woman and lesbian in quotation marks. That's one way to communicate that those words don't fit. Although I feel like maybe I'm stating the problem too lightly. How would you describe it?

PRIEST: [...]

Mmhmm. Yeah. So, another way to pose my question is hmm. Well, this will seem reductive. Did the linguistic turn result in an incredibly painful form of entrapment?

PRIEST: [...]

Um, okay. To be honest, I guess what I'm talking about is—whatever, I want to talk about my experience as a student in the graduate program. Sorry.

PRIEST: [...]

Sure, thanks. Okay. Well, I guess I thought This is so twisted and impossible. Because if I take this stuff seriously, if I take theory seriously and go on to live out my life surrounded by people who are serious about theory, then at best I'll get to live my life in relation to a sentence. I'm a woman in quotation marks. That is the best world they'll offer to me. And I'll be required to accept the offer with pleasure. It will be the price of admission for every conversation. I'll have to be willing to perform nonequivalence with a sign I might not even want, with pleasure.

PRIEST: [...]

I think it felt like torture to me. I don't know, I was like why is this even the point? For some reason it was the saddest thing to imagine that one day, maybe at the end of my life, I'll be able to say with delighted conviction that I know how to read and I'm a woman in quotation marks.

PRIEST: [...]

I know, but that's not really what I'm talking about. I get what you're saying. But I'm not talking about that.

PRIEST: [...]

No, what I'm saying is I don't think it's pleasurable. I think it's painful when you don't like being a woman and the best you can do with that feeling is you can put the signifier in quotation marks.

PRIEST: [...]

I know. I see. I don't really disagree with you.

PRIEST: [...]

Well yeah. Then sometimes, like, when you're having a conversation, there's this totally uncanny feeling. It's like your interlocutor has gone and lent you a depth that isn't—it's like you have two depths. You have the one your interlocutor is giving to you and the one you're giving to yourself. I think for the entirety of my time in the graduate program, the depth you gave me belonged to Andrea Dworkin.

PRIEST: [...]

I'm serious! I felt like there was no way for me to show you your mistake. You were the one with the authority to grant depths and pin words to surfaces. It never worked when I tried to do it back to you, or to the others on my committee. It was impossible to do to others what was being done to me.

PRIEST: [...]

I think so, yeah.

PRIEST: [...]

I'm still ashamed. I'm still thinking about it, which is embarrassing. I'm a professor. I shouldn't be obsessing over what happened in grad school. I mean, why do you think I'm talking to you? I said I wanted to interview you about your book, but what I need is something else. Closure? Or recognition? I honestly don't know when I'll stop thinking about whatever the hell happened to me in grad school. Hopefully one day I will? I don't know.

PRIEST: [...]

But I was playing. That's what I thought. I thought I was playing. I think you guys were taking me too seriously. Or maybe your version of play read as anxiety and torture to me, and my version of play read as displeasure and disobedience to you?

PRIEST: [...]

I don't think I understood what the committee was asking of me. I was able to sense the pressure of the demand, but I don't think I understood what it was or why it was given to me. I didn't have the perspective.

PRIEST: [...]

One of the things you wanted from me, I think, was a mirror for your pleasure. It was never a matter of making mine legible. Liking the same things in the same ways, that's what it meant to be smart in that program.

PRIEST: [...]

But none of us were being smart! What was happening was I wasn't liking the text in the preferred way.

PRIEST: [...]

Okay, but that's confusing. Because if you were asking me in good faith to buy into your paradigm, if you honestly wanted me to approach literary analysis as some kind of sex, then why wasn't it fair for me to say Okay, fine, but you should know I don't have sex like you do. I'm a sadist.

PRIEST: [...]

I kept thinking Oh my god, I'm going to have to learn how to be a masochist. Or else my professors are going to deem me an idiot and derail my life! That was really depressing. I got so depressed. I couldn't get up. After a point, I couldn't get up anymore. That's why I kept failing my comps.

PRIEST: [...]

But the reality is I was playing just like you were, but differently? Whatever. I guess now I know that I never want to do that to a student. I will never demand that a student produce my enjoyment for me.

PRIEST: [...]

Yeah, true.

PRIEST: [...]

Yeah.

PRIEST: [...]

I remember there was one professor who wouldn't allow me to leave the classroom. I was the last one in there. I was packing up my shit, and he went and stood in the doorway. He wouldn't let me pass until I told him what I really wanted from the texts.

PRIEST: [...]

I was thirty years old. Would you trap a thirty-year-old adult in a classroom?

PRIEST: [...]

Yeah. Okay. I get what you're saying.

PRIEST: [...]

Do you know what scandal this conversation brings to mind?

PRIEST: [...]

Yes, bingo. So you've been following it.

PRIEST: [...]

Would you want to talk about it?

PRIEST: [...]

Oh good. What's your take?

PRIEST: [...]

Mmmmmmm.

PRIEST: [...]

Mmhmm. Mmhmm.

PRIEST: [...]

Wow. Well, for whatever it's worth, I don't see her as another gay person. I mean, right?

PRIEST: [...]

Yeah, the guy's gay.

PRIEST: [...]

Okay, sure. Queer.

PRIEST: [...]

I know, fair enough.

PRIEST: [...]

Ha, yeah, *Bully Bloggers* ran a ton.

PRIEST: [...]

I guess I get a kick out of those defenses. They're like *What you don't understand, scandalized audience, is how to read!*

PRIEST: [...]

I think it's fascinating how post-structuralist theories about reading supplied the discourse those academics called upon. It's as if they really believed that deconstruction would exonerate her. Deconstruction and intimidation.

PRIEST: [...]

Come on, they tried to deconstruct the *Times* article. They tried to deconstruct the legal brief.

PRIEST: [...]

But he was never into her. That's what was so disturbing to them. That all those layers of anxious uncertainty could be so easily reduced. It was disturbing to them. Turns out he didn't love her. He never loved her. He was faking it. The sum of his enjoyment was no greater than the function of her authority.

PRIEST: […]

Well, I guess maybe my point is it seems unfair to apply the paradigm of sexual seduction to acts of literary analysis within a pedagogical setting. It's difficult to differentiate between seduction and coercion in the classroom—or is that the point for you?

PRIEST: […]

Because good students cannot betray that they aren't seduced by the professor's analysis. Were they to do that, they'd be bad students. Good students are seduced, or they appear to be seduced, from the professor's vantage. That means the game is fun, not because it's a game you can lose, but because it's an anxious, heady trip. You can never be sure of the operative force. Is it desire or authority?

PRIEST: […]

I'm guessing I seemed like a blockhead. Or like I was frigid? Indifferent to the curriculum. Too simple-minded to know I should be faking it. Or too stubborn to give you what you wanted. Maybe there's some truth in all of that. But still, you can't put a student like that in front of a committee of professors without some kind of collective hysterical breakdown happening.

PRIEST: […]

I was a student who wasn't seduced by literary theory. I think, by not being seduced, I was effectively shaming the professors on my committee. Because within this pedagogical paradigm, which is a game of seduction, you experienced something that felt like sexual rejection. That sort of thing can be shaming.

PRIEST: [...]

Well, sometimes people with authority become hysterical when they're ashamed. They get angry. Then they get vindictive. You guys punished me. Everybody got so upset because I seemed to be incapable of taking pleasure in the text. That was literally the note I got the first time I failed my comps. I was like Okay I'll fuck the text harder. No amount of seduction or persuasion or intimidation was going to work on me.

PRIEST: [...]

I should've faked it. But was I capable of faking it, I don't know. Probably not. I don't know why all of this is so grotesque to me. I'm having trouble just explaining it to you. I think it embarrasses me to say it. For me to have performed some kind of submission to the text, like, in a way that would've adequately signified yes, I am finding this pleasurable—no, I couldn't do that. I was too fragile to do that. Plus, what if I had started to believe it. I felt like I had too much at stake to start believing it, even though I couldn't name the stakes. You could've held a gun to my head. I wouldn't have been able to name them. Why do you think that is? If my degree was the only thing on the line, then how come I didn't just fake it? Why didn't I decide to at least try to give you what you wanted?

PRIEST: [...]

I guess all of us could've come clean and admitted that there are many ways to enjoy. But then we would've proved the existence of a bigger world. With many pleasures in it. Some of them yours, some of them mine.

PRIEST: [...]

If the planet were to become uninhabitable and you were forced to pack up and move to a novel, would you really choose to live in *Venus in Furs*? Because I'd choose *120 Days of Sodom*. *Venus in Furs* is, like, one of many paragraphs in *120 Days*. There's enough room for both of us to live in that book.

PRIEST: [...]

I sort of want to ask why it is that enjoyment should be the measure of a student's education, but what I'm trying to communicate is yes, I took your paradigm seriously. I think I took it as seriously as you did. I'm taking it seriously now. The vitriol I provoked in the members of my committee suggests a scene of sexual rejection. I mean, why did you guys care so much that I failed my comps? If I just wasn't very smart as far as graduate students go, then so what. That's no reason for anyone to get hysterical.

PRIEST: [...]

Yeah.

PRIEST: [...]

Yeah. Yeah.

PRIEST: [...]

Joke's on me.

PRIEST: [...]

No, that was the committee's verdict. Joke's on me.

PRIEST: [...]

It's what I was told when it was over, in an email.

PRIEST: [...]

I studied comedy for three years. Then I spent three months trying to pass an exam that was meant to last three days, despite everyone recognizing it was kind of killing me—my girlfriend said someone called her to ask was I alive or should somebody maybe break into my apartment—and then, finally and at last, you told me to stop and called me the butt of the joke. When I read that email, I was like Holy shit. I passed my comps? But where does butt of the joke fall on the grading scale! Whatever. I printed it out. If I ever publish another book, I want to turn it into a blurb.

PRIEST: [...]

I don't know. Do you want me to read it to you?

PRIEST: [...]

I'm happy to report the committee has unanimously agreed on a low pass for your essay. There was a unanimous joy in watching your mind exercise itself, but there was also a general sense that your argument was encased in a set of propositions it couldn't liquidly offer, ride, or self-reflexively challenge. As one member wrote, it seems as if your argument just can't recognize the joke of it all. It's a joke on you, and on all of us, and one that defines the first as well as the final insight of deconstruction. We want what we can't have, and by defining what we want we guarantee we can't have it. Hearty congratulations. When you've had a day or two to catch your breath, let's put our heads together to discuss the next and final steps toward that PhD.

PRIEST: [...]

Really? By defining what we want, we guarantee we can't have it? What a thing to say to a student. What is that? Not a pedagogy!

PRIEST: [...]

Sure, the joke is on all of us. But only one of us sucks at school. Only one of us is naïve enough to blurt out what they want.

PRIEST: [...]

I never wanted to become theory's butt. I thought I was studying to be the comedian!

PRIEST: [...]

I wasn't trying to outwit deconstruction. Want to know what I think about deconstruction? I think it's a kink repackaged as universal law. I think it's an anxious attempt to get off while drowning in an unnameable sorrow. Or it's one way to hide from yourself as your fading life is wasted. I understand there's no outwitting it. I just like to exercise my will.

PRIEST: [...]

Well. I was thoroughly humiliated. You won.

PRIEST: [...]

It's okay. I'm kind of trying to say that I'm glad it happened. It helped me to see that I was—that I couldn't define what I wanted. I couldn't even name it. People would ask me what I wanted to eat, and I would say I have no idea.

PRIEST: [...]

But I do. I do hope you can get what you want. Isn't that what magic is for? Or what's a prayer? Why do people pray?

PRIEST: [...]

Did I ever tell you about my process for writing the dissertation? I spent a year reading Derrida's essays. Like, I'd read a single essay twenty times in a row. I wanted to get all of it into my body. That way, whenever I sat down to write, I'd be able to channel Jacques Derrida at will. At the time I was in this—well, it was a graduate-student support group for women. There was one session where everyone was talking about writing the dissertation. I was describing my research because I hadn't started writing. I said I just finished reading another essay by Derrida for the thirtieth time and now I think I'm ready to start writing the novel. I asked if they'd let me try out the voice. They told me that would be fine, so I began to perform some Derrida for them, and everyone in the group was looking at me like—I don't know, their mouths were open. But these were STEM people. I guess I was thinking these people have no idea how weird English Studies is. I paused to ask What's wrong, and one of them said Oh god, you're covered in hives.

PRIEST: […]

No, to me it was the perfect sign. I was ready to write. I ate so much Derrida, I got hives. I'd never gotten hives before. But ever since that moment in that stupid women's-support group, I've gotten them. I get them all the time now. I'm a person who gets hives. I took the text inside with so much zeal, it produced a signifier on the surface of my skin. That's what you wanted.

PRIEST: […]

II. A SENTIMENTAL EDUCATION

Dear Committee,

I am writing to submit my dissertation manuscript. I've been calling it a novel. In terms of word count, however, it's a novella but shorter. They call that a novelette. So it's a novelette. It's a sentimental novelette in stories. It's possessed by my own spirit and the spirit of Marquis de Sade.

I *love* Marquis de Sade. I think he's the only person I would die for. Unfortunately, he's already dead. I want to talk to him, but I don't know how to speak French and he's dead. That's why I'm inconsolable. I really love Marquis de Sade.

In what's left of his journals from Charenton, there's a chapter-by-chapter outline for a novel. It looks like it would've been an incredible book. Sade never wrote it because he died. One of the chapters has the sparest notation: delicious force. That's where I got the title for my dissertation.

I'll place printed copies of the manuscript in your campus mailboxes this week. Also, sometime before my defense takes place, I will email you a proper, semi-intelligent account of the project in the form of an abstract. My defense is on May 17 at 3:00 p.m.

Thank you for reading.

Thank you for enduring my nature and compelling me to learn.

R

Autobiographical Animal

Jacques was a person in history.

Jacques had a little cat.

One day, the little cat crept into the bathroom while Jacques was bathing. The cat walked up to the tub, sat down on the floor, and watched. Naturally, Jacques was naked. Jacques saw the cat see his nakedness, and Jacques felt shame. The shame was unusual because it was complex. The complexity took a long time to unpack when Jacques told the story to a room of scholars in 1997. The story was original and emotional. It was humbling and pathetic, but not too pathetic. Jacques's story, the scholars argued, was appropriately pathetic. Also, the story was lovely. It was a lovely, lovely story. But it wasn't true. I know because I was there. In the bathroom. Next to the cat. Jacques did not account for my presence.

Throughout the history of the West, people have treated animals like garbage. The difference Jacques makes is: he said he felt bad.

Jacques felt shame.

He was naked. He'd been bathing. Now he was ready to exit the bathtub. He rose to a standing position and issued the signal. He used one of his tan fingers, which was bent and dripping, to point at the towel on the rack. Except he didn't point at the towel on the rack. The rack was bare.

Fuck, shit. Where was the towel?

Fuck my face off my head. Run a sword through my neck because I'm an asshole. I'm an asshole and I'm stupid. I'm so fucking stupid—

The towel was in the dryer.

The towel was in the dryer, and the dryer was in the laundry. The laundry was in the alcove, which connected to the kitchen, at the opposite end of the estate. Be right back. I turned, and I ran.

What is a TA?

The stick isn't universal, you know. It's not even standard. It's his, and you don't really know him, do you? No, I think you do not. You know the one you serve. You know the one you serve, and I know the one I serve, and the sticks are different. How can I present myself to you without disappearing behind the shadow that is cast by the thought your master built in the miserable fist of your vision? You'll have to take me at my word when I tell you what I am.

I'm worthless.

Some days get fucked, so what. There wasn't a towel on the rack, and I suppose there was nothing to be done about it—no action under the fucked-open sun to make up for the one I should've remembered to accomplish an hour earlier, i.e., retrieve the towel from the dryer and return it to the rack.

Jesus, fuck. The TA handles basic tasks, okay? Such as grading papers or working directly for any professor who by virtue of excessive fame and/or age requires day-to-day assistance and emotional support—and I told him not to worry, didn't I? I told him to stay put.

Jacques, I said, I'm going to the laundry to get the towel. I'll be back in a jiffy.

Well, no. I didn't use the word jiffy. I would never use that word. I cite it now because it's kind of cute and very casual, and that's the way I want you to see me. That's what feels comfortable, you understand.

I ran in the direction of the laundry, which connected to the kitchen, and since I'd already fucked up the day I stopped at the fridge and grabbed a can of beer. The beer was a Dale's Pale Ale. I really liked that beer. I stored some in Jacques's refrigerator. Jacques didn't care and he never touched it. He didn't drink much at the end of his life.

I went outside to the patio by way of the sliding door in the breakfast nook. I sipped the beer. I smoked a cigarette. The cigarette was an American Spirit from the goldenrod pack.

Upon reentering the house, I felt looser. The beer had mattered because I hadn't eaten. Plus, I'd already ruined the day, and the ruining felt like relief, you understand, so I strode like Goliath over the expanse of the kitchen to the alcove with the laundry in it, feeling good in the place where my body was meant to exist, or where it supposedly endured, or whatever. It wasn't there.

The towel was right where I'd left it. It was sitting in the dryer, which gave me an idea. I should warm the towel in the dryer. If I warmed the towel in the dryer, then I'd produce time, perhaps ten minutes or more, which means I could have another beer and I could smoke again.

There's no such thing as a good decision, right? Plus, Jacques would stay where I'd left him. He didn't want to slip on the way out of the tub, not again. He was waiting for my help. Clenched and curved, he was probably cold and very angry. Cold anger should be enough to make a man want a warm towel. I'd want a warm towel. I speculated that Jacques would want one, too. Meanwhile, the cat was just watching him. The cat was spying on the shape of his sex.

Spying on the shape of his sex. That's how Jacques talked. I should mention that I didn't care for Jacques's language. I didn't care for the body of his work. I loathed the entirety of his scholarship, pretty much. It itched me. All the time, I was itching.

What. It's not like the wait would kill him. Do you need me to say it outright? I was not trying to kill Jacques Derrida. I'm a fiction writer.

I write short novels that are technically short stories that resemble scholarly essays about literature, but given the state of the academic job market, see—

Whatever, fuck you.

This story is not an impotent attempt to channel Poe.

Okay, Poe's an influence for sure. I'm drawn to the style, mostly the hair and the coats. The neckties are a turnoff, but I love the pants in that photo. The one where he's holding hands with the model skeleton?

Look. I wasn't equipped to pull a Poe. I was a TA, you understand. I was a loser who wanted to be looser. I wanted to be a looser loser, so I activated the dryer, setting the timer for fifteen minutes, then I grabbed another beer from the fridge, strode like Goliath to the patio, smoked a cigarette, et cetera. When I returned to the bathroom, I saw the cat. The bit about the cat is true. Jacques never lied about the cat. The cat was watching, and Jacques was blushing. I had the warm towel in my arms, and I presented it to Jacques: my arms with the towel draped over. I held out that entire apparatus, and Jacques grabbed onto it. That's how he maintained his balance.

He lifted one foot up and over the lip of the tub. Rachel, he said.

I was calling myself Rachel then.

Maybe it was due to his accent? I don't know. Whenever Jacques said Rachel, he managed to cram the name into a single syllable. He made the name sound like a curse. It was like he said Fuck! And yeah, I love the name Fuck. If I didn't have a quote unquote career—well, if I didn't need it, you know, the money, which I funnel into the rent and all the fucking foods that only serve to prolong the youth of it, the youth of the husk, and the husk will not end, the husk will not end, and by now it should've ended, I swear, it should've ended, but it hasn't ended because it endures, it endures, endures, et cetera—I'd change my name to Fuck.

I really love that name.

The body of Jacques was much colder than I'd wagered it would be. It was remarkably inflexible, so I helped Jacques walk to the closet. Then I invited him to point at the trousers he wanted. I pulled the trousers from the hanger and up and over the lower half of Jacques—and Jacques wore slacks, mind you, high-end slacks, which were not ideal to work with, even on days that didn't get fucked, so—whatever, Jacques couldn't be bent, okay? Like, his joints. They were not operative.

And yet, I triumphed. I dressed Jacques. Then I told him that he really should, at this advanced point in his career, you know—I said he should consider getting himself a pair of joggers.

Joggers are user-friendly menswear (pants) that have elastic bands at the ankles and waist. They are baggy, yes, but not in a way that looks bad on a person. They're baggy in a way that's comfortable and forgiving and easy. I think joggers look great, I said. I'd had a lot of beers and spoke at length on the greatness of joggers. In conclusion, I said, joggers look great. They are great. They're fucking great, and we could get you a pair. We could get two pairs, Jacques.

Jacques frowned. He said he had work to do.

That's okay, I said. I told him he could work.

You're wrong, said Jacques. I can work or I can go get joggers. I cannot do both.

But you can do both, I said, because you have me.

Jacques said—

Okay, basically, Jacques replied that one cannot acquire slacks without going to the store and trying them on. That's what he took issue with, trying them on. Jacques didn't have time to try them on because he had to work.

Joggers come in three sizes, I replied. Don't you get it? You don't have to try them on.

No, Jacques did not get it. He was dumb, totally dumb. Every time he slipped into that stuck state, I would find myself wanting to handle him like an old console. To just hit him, you know, with the flat of my palm.

Three. Sizes. Period, I continued. Fuck man, I'm telling you the truth. The pants will fit. They'll look great on you. Plus, they'll be so easy for you to manage by yourself. To pull them up, see? I mimed Jacques pulling them up all by himself. And they'll look fucking great.

Fine, Jacques said. Take my card. Get yourself a pair, too. I think you need joggers.

No, I said. I think you need joggers.

No, you need joggers, he said.

You need joggers, I said. Then I said—

Well okay, what I did next was I attempted to explain that I did not need joggers by explicating the difference between want and need.

Then I realized Jacques understands the difference between want and need because Jacques is a philosopher. Well, he was basically a philosopher-adjacent person, according to some people. In any case, I reasoned, if there's a person inside this closet who doesn't understand the difference between want and need, then that person isn't Jacques. That person is me, probably. Therefore, reality is, it's somewhat likely that I don't understand anything, including whatever Jacques is saying.

Turns out, Jacques was saying he could see my want. He saw I wanted joggers. He was offering to pay for them, the joggers—which, hello, he should pay for them, absolutely. I made $16,000 a year because I worked for Jacques.

Cool, cool. I did a little bow. I didn't mean to do it. May I borrow your car?

Go, he nodded. I must read now.

Then I laughed in his face. Because Jacques didn't read. Jacques never read.

Jacques placed opened books on tabletops, yes, but he didn't look at them. What he did was he paced wildly in their general vicinity for five hours whilst kicking and stepping on the cat—which, okay, that much is obvious, right? I mean, you've read Jacques's work. It's obvious. He never read anything. He didn't give a shit about animals.

Okay.

I took the card and the car. I drove to Target. I bought, like, eight pairs of joggers and a case of Dale's Pale Ale.

Jacques and I wore the same size in joggers. Therefore, we shared the pants until the day he died. Or look, whatever, I wore some of them. I was right. They looked fine on him. They looked fucking great. I was grateful. So yeah, I want to use this time to thank him. I want to thank him and pay homage and—

I was a TA, fuck you. Jacques didn't tell the truth because Jacques was vain. I hated him. I hated his entire body of work. I hated working for him because it permanently reduced my earning potential, and I had zero family to bail me out, which was terrible because it was terrifying, but I will not make my fear your burden because you don't care. You don't care, and yet you know. You know the only job a person can get once they've been a TA is—well, they can be a TA again, basically. The pay is shit. Sometimes they don't have enough for the rent—and I'm tenure-track, mind you.

Still, I believe it is necessary to give thanks because that's the protocol, you understand. Plus, sure, I did want them. I wanted the joggers. I'm being serious. When was the last time someone like Jacques—you know, someone who controls every aspect of your life and your death and your pay—what I'm saying is has someone like Jacques ever given something to you? No, not just something. Has a person like Jacques ever given you the thing you wanted?

Yes, this story is stupid!

Jacques said I could use his car and his credit card to get some joggers, and I got the joggers. That's my story. My story is stupid. In contrast, Jacques's story is false. Jacques wasn't honest, you see, and—

Whatever, he died.

The death wasn't noble. I was there for that, too. I never liked his style. Jacques wasn't Poe. Jacques wasn't Poe because Jacques wasn't smart, and he wasn't talented, and his proclivities were mainstream, and he never read a single book. But fine, none of this is news to you because you've read Jacques's books. I've read Jacques's books. I've read everything.

I'm serious. I've read everything. They pay me shit.

Okay, Jacques is dead. Also, Jacques was wrong. Jacques was wrong about sex because he was dumb. But, once upon a time, his money got me joggers, and I wore the joggers. It felt good. It still feels good. Because it exists. Supposedly, it exists. It exists. It endures. Or whatever, it's just there. It's there, all right? It's there. So thanks. Thank you. Thanks.

Pay me shit and give me tenure now.

No, no. It's not possible.

Seminar XXXXXXIVX: Rats in the Maze at the School of Love

What is mysticism? We learn about mysticism from individuals who are bright, educated, and creative. Mystics are curious about limits. The punk's pink tongue tests the sheet of bubblegum, and he wants to shoot himself over the threshold. I'm talking about having an orgasm, ladies and gentlemen. But you know that. The smart ones get it.

The mystic rides the thin, folded horse right up to the border where knowledge meets stupidity. You've seen it. I know you've seen it. You've seen it in the park. The park or another egalitarian space. Take your pick. They're disappearing, by the way. Those spaces where all are welcome. Goodbye!

[GENERAL LAUGHTER]

You're in the park at the end of history, wearing a virile blouse, and everything is verdant. Everything is green. The chatter on the telly, the mediatization of the massive brain of man, the ingredient list on the little box of what's-it-called. Fruits and grains. Help me out, folks. [AUDIBLE BREATHING] Cereal, yes. Ladies and gentlemen, I am talking about a box of cereal. Plus, fascism. Nazis. [COUGHS]

xxxxxx

That bit makes me cringe. I have to kill it. But I'll tell you what happened.

What I was doing up there is I was trying to compose a stand-up routine by mashing up Jacques Lacan and Jacques Derrida. I was mashing Jacques and Jacques the way you used to do it when you'd ram the Barbies together. I was doing something like that.

I don't know. I drafted the story a long time ago. I was writing my dissertation. I was doing it windowless, in a room underground. Because by this point in my life, I'd tried lesbianism. I tried it. Then I decided to live underneath my landlord's house.

I lived under my landlord's house.

I read.

I wrote.

Also, I watched YouTube. I watched videos of Jacques Lacan and Jacques Derrida. I took screenshots of the faces, the faces of Jacques and Jacques. Then I searched Google for old-fashioned drawings

of hymens. I took screenshots of those, too. I used a cheap pho-
to-editing app to superimpose the hymens over the faces.

See?

el sujeto se supone que sabe.

(Now I'm simplifying what novels are about), I'm not capable of talking in generalities about love.

That's Georges Bataille on the bottom left.

Okay. I did it to Bataille, too.

Look, I did it to a lot of people. All the time I was doing that. Also, I was transcribing audio recordings of lectures about literary theory because—I don't know what was going on with my life or why I was having one.

My landlord owned a dozen properties in Salt Lake City. His name was Bob. I met him through my ex, back when I was trying lesbianism. He was my ex's landlord. He told me I could live under his family's house. It was the house he shared with his adult sons. Bob said I could live in the house, but under it and with his adult sons, for a reduced price, which was nice of Bob. Rent was expensive in Salt Lake City. I couldn't afford it. Also, I was bad at lesbianism. Well, Bob didn't know that.

Nobody knew that.

My dad didn't know it. Because I lied to him. I called him up and told him everything is fine because it's just lesbianism. My dad always told me everything's probably fine because it's probably just lesbianism. Sure, okay. That's why I called him and told him how it felt. It felt fine. It felt right. Lesbianism feels right? It feels fucking great is what I said. Then I asked if he wanted to know about something else that feels great.

Um. Maybe, he said.

No one has to worry about me anymore. Tell the others. Tell them they can stop worrying about me now. No worries. Just lesbianism. Fucking great. Tell them.

Naturally, my dad told me congrats. He said it was wonderful news. Wonderful news, the lesbianism. Congrats. Forget about the others. They forgot you were living or that you ever were born. But thank you for the reminder. It's a helpful tip.

Want to see something from one of the lectures I was transcribing?

I'm not a woman. But I'm a feminist. So I am a woman? And I'm a lesbian. But I didn't want to be a lesbian. I thought I was a straight man, but then I turned out to be a lesbian. Okay, fine. Also, at the end of the day, I'm the Good Gay. You know what I mean. I play that part. The Good Gay for the university. I'm also a woman. Also, a lesbian. And a female professor, not a male one. Even though I told them I'm not a woman. I told them I never was a woman. I never wanted to be a woman, but I never transitioned either, so I'm not a trans person in that particular way—that's what Derrida means! That complexity is the meaning of deconstruction!

Aaaaaaaah-ha-ha.

When I had nowhere to live and Bob told me I could live in his basement, with his adult sons, I seized the deal. I got to watch YouTube and didn't have to pay for internet. Maybe that's because Bob had already figured internet into my rent, which was very fair and cheap for Salt Lake City. It was $575 a month. Either way, it felt like I was getting something for free. Namely, internet access. YouTube.

The way Bob saw it, I was entitled to access the service because I was living in his family's house. I guess I began to see it that way, too. I felt like I was part of the family's house. Like, I was a structural feature that happened to be in the basement. Because I did have to keep to the basement at all times. That was fine.

I kept to it.

I watched YouTube. I captured the hymens and faces. I superimposed the hymens over the faces. I've gone underground to work on the collages for my creative-writing dissertation is what I said. No one had asked where I went.

The wall behind the couch had a person-shaped hole in it. One time, while I was working on my collages, Bob came down to the basement to look upon the hole. He stood before the hole and stared emotively at it, like he was paying his respects.

He said: That poor man.

And I said: That poor guy.

He said: That poor, poor man.

And I said: That poor, poor guy.

He said: That poor man fell into the wall.

And I said: That poor guy. Fell into the wall?

He said: The poor man. He fell into the wall.

I said: Okay but how bad was it. I mean. He got out.

Poor man. Poor, poor man.

Bob.

He fell into the wall. That poor man.

Bob. Tell me he's not still in there.

Poor man fell into the wall.

Lie to me, Bob. There's no man in the wall. No man in the wall, Bob. The man fell into the wall, yes, the poor guy, I know that part by heart, but then the man walked out of the wall. The man walked out of the wall and exited the greater Salt Lake area. Now he's a well-adjusted adult. The man is a happy, financially secure, well-adjusted adult, Bob. That whole episode with the wall, it's just a dream to him. It's an old nightmare, Bob. The wall is not where the man currently resides. There's no man in the wall, Bob. No man in the wall. Bob. Bob. Bob. Bob, please. The poor guy.

Bob was quiet. He was in a trance, an emotional trance. Or he was guarding something. He was keeping watch over it. It was the person-shaped hole in the wall.

Bob came to by way of a jolt that rollicked his body and his hairs. Yeah, it was as if someone near the ceiling, like a winged cherub or just a human person—because the truth is the basement ceiling was so low you could touch it very easily just by standing, nobody needed wings, not at all—even I couldn't take my T-shirt off without scraping my elbows bloody—but okay, someone near the ceiling, with or without wings, used an index finger to burst the fat, wet bubble of thought that was floating overhead of Bob. That's when Bob regained consciousness. He glanced around the way birds glance around when they land to gobble crumbs. Bob glanced at the four corners of the basement. He told me the place looked great. It didn't look great and it wasn't a place. I was doing such a good job with the place, he said. The place was total shit. Bob smiled. He turned and climbed the stairs.

Bye Bob.

Bob was nice to me.

If I were to rework the opening bit about mystics and cereal, I think I'd probably spend more time on the blouses. Jacques Lacan wore hysterical blouses. I know this from watching YouTube. Lacan's blouses had flowers and sashes and bows and ribbons and other kinds of shit all over them. I can tell Lacan thought the blouses were very virile, but I don't think they were actually virile. That's a compelling conflict for a short work of literary fiction. If I were to rewrite the opening bit, which I won't because it was such an embarrassing bit, I'd stage the conflict around a disagreement over the meaning of the blouses. Also, the wigs. Lacan liked wigs.

Lacan liked blouses, wigs, mysticism, and math.

The wigs are connected to the fact that Lacan was a notorious hair puller. It was just part of his practice. It was simply a portion of his methodology, as an analyst. Lacan pulled hairs. I like to imagine that clients were hip to the technique. That's why they wore wigs to therapy. Cheap ones, too. Why waste a good wig on shitty therapy? That's a saying. Whenever the client wore the wig, Lacan was prevented from pulling actual, biological hairs. He'd grab the wig instead. The wig would pop off the top like a cork. Then Lacan would slip it into a briefcase and carry it home. That's how the collection began. Lacan had a formidable wig collection. He wasn't comfortable with his image. The poor guy.

I had a lot of waking nightmares during my time in Bob's basement because I didn't sleep. I had to do my dreaming consciously. I dreamt about the hole in the wall. I had this one dream that played against my will. I couldn't make it stop. I couldn't stop thinking the dream. It had to do with Don Quixote. Fuck you, all my professors were obsessed with *Don Quixote*.

Don Quixote was climbing through the hole in the wall, one thin leg at a time. Like a syrup-drenched spider, he was threadlike and graceful and impossibly slow. He was entering my world. I was lying on the couch, watching it happen. I didn't move my body. I didn't move my body because I was familiar with the logic that governed the scene. Movement made things real. It made everything real.

I was thirty years old, which is embarrassing. To dream that way at thirty.

This bit deserves to die.

Think of the scene from *The Shining*. Think it slower. Ninety times slower. Quixote was pushing his head through the hole in the wall. Slowly. By languid degrees. I was paralyzed on the couch, and Quixote was looking at me but not seeing me. Because he was seeing her, you understand. That's his whole shtick. He was seeing

Dulcinea. That's what made it so I couldn't move at all. Yes, I tried to think about something else. Lesbianism, mysticism, blouses. Things I could do with Bob's sons. The sons didn't want to do anything.

It's okay.

Bob had two adult sons. What they liked was to take off their shirts and lie on their beds. Their beds had plaid bedspreads that looked so vintage. The sons loved to lounge on their beds with their long, blond hairs fanned out on the vintage bedspreads. I swear it felt just like the '70s. I'd never been to the '70s. Somehow, I knew what the '70s felt like. The sons were tan and healthy. All the colors were muted in a lovely way. It was just like the '70s. I was pretty lonely.

The stand-up routine I wrote by ramming Jacques and Jacques like Barbies embarrasses me. It cracked jokes about rats in mazes and feminine jouissance. I don't like it anymore.

I still like the title, I guess.

I think the rats were supposed to be symbols. They stood for the women. Lacan and Derrida liked talking about women. I can't let you see those parts, but I'll show you how the bit ends.

xxxxxx

Mystics are different. They're not so fixated on the literal. They're enrolled in classes at college. They know how to read. They've taken the book to heart, and who among us can bear to deny them the sweet Spanish knight? He's riding to you on a thin, folded horse. The sweet Spanish knight. Once he has started, there are no words to make him stop. [SLURPS DRINK] There you have it: no rape, no murder.

[GENERAL LAUGHTER]

A philosopher named Jacques Derrida once wrote *perpetual, the rape* to erotically demonstrate how there is no such thing as finishing, which means there is no such thing as mastery, which means there is no such thing as mastery via rape, which is true, aye, it is true, and yet, as far as the Other is concerned, the threat is not immaterial. Death isn't entirely out of the question. Death, actual death, it happens. What is the actual meaning of mastery? My friends, there is none!

Derrida loved to talk about Mallarmé. The man loved to talk about Mallarmé. He told me Mallarmé went to see a clown do a show in a barn. Mallarmé? In a barn? Come on. Yet I wonder, might we take a moment to indulge this sweet, sensitive, seductive fantasy? Of Mallarmé with a clown in a barn? The clown contorts his gorgeous body in a dance of contempt, mimesis, and love. Unspeakable, immense is the pleasure that belongs to Mallarmé.

[EXTENDED PAUSE]

Mallarmé did the right thing afterward, folks. He put the pleasure in the text. Oh, my friends, to hold that text! To touch its surface, together, with Jacques Derrida!!

The text has a body, my friends.

Oh.

My.

God.

The text has a body.

Come, let us kneel.

[S L O W   F L A T U L E N C E]

Actual, biological death happens. It happens in history, which is fiction. It happens in barns. It happens in poor neighborhoods, as Lévi-Strauss has wisely observed.

Aye.

We've known since Nietzsche that the Other experiences enjoyment by faking enjoyment, whether it is in mortal danger or no. Freud, working hard in the men's rights movement, managed to anchor this oddity to the bedrock of culture/science. Now, thanks to the long-standing tradition of reading and writing, we find ourselves hovering over the site of a massive breakthrough.

[EXTENDED PAUSE]

The only kind of sexual organ that exists is the phallus, which does not mean the penis, as Freud makes clear, unless we were to talk of a penis with the remarkable characteristic of not admitting to a vagina.

[GENERAL LAUGHTER]

The idea of an organ in glorious monadic isolation. Namely, the penis. Or, more precisely, the penis in its privileged state of tumescence and erection. This point is worth stopping at.

[PAUSE]

Ladies and gentlemen, mystics are very unusual and complex. They know it well, the limit where knowledge meets stupidity. [LAUGHTER, LAUGHTER, BURP] Mystics know how to play like the elites. Using innate abilities to do math, science, and common sense, mystics have devised an intricate state-of-the-art machinery to milk human fragility for all the social capital and somatic ecstasy it is worth. But what does it mean?

It means friendship.

It means ethics, which means friendship.

Friendship. Friendship. Ethics.

Fashions come and go, but what of mystics?

Mystics evolve.

Mystics read, write, learn, love, eat, grow, fuck, play with wigs, and do mysticism.

Mystics evolve.

Mystics evolve.

Mystics evolve. Mystics evolve.

Mystics evolve, despite—

Despite.

Despite.

Despite, I won't say their phallus.

Despite what encumbers them and goes by that name.

To each his own. His very own-----

very own----His very own-----

His very------

His---very own-----very own----His---own---His---

His---

His, his----his---his

His---his----his---

His---

His----his,

His---his---his-----

His---

His---

His---

His-------------

His---His---His----His---,   his---His---His---His---His-
--His---His---His---, his---His---, his---His---, his---,
his---His---His---His---His---His---His---His---His---,

his---His---, his---His---, his---, his---His---His---, his---,
his---His---, his---, his---, his---, his---, his---, his---His-
---His---, his---His---, his---, his---His---His---His---
His---His---His---His---His---, his---His---, his---His---,
his---, his---His---His---, his---, his---His---, his---, his---,
his---, his---, his---, his---His--- His---, his---His---, his---
, his---His---His---His---His---His---His---His---His---,
his---His---, his---His---, his---, his---His---his---His---
his---, his---His---, his---, his---, his---, his---, his---, his---
His----His---, his---His---, his---, his---His---His---His---
His---His---His---His---His---, his---His---, his---His---,
his---, his---His---His---, his---, his---His---, his---, his---,
his---, his---, his---, his---His----His---, his---His---, his---
, his---His---His---His---His---His---His---His---His---,
his---His---, his---His---, his---, his---His---His---, his---,
his---His---, his---, his---, his---, his---, his---, his---His----

"Alone you created the man. Now, together, we will create his mate."

Severin

Severin is a character in a novel.

He's a Galician gentleman and landowner. He is thirty years old, a smoker. He is sexually inexperienced. He craves eggs, soft boiled, and likes to press his face against statues. He likes statues. He loves fur. He dabbles in poetry and science. He collects animal skeletons, stuffed birds, and plastic cats. He does not want to be hanged by a woman, so he trains women. He rests his chin in his hands. His hands are delicately veined.

According to his neighbors, Severin is dangerous and odd. Severin has zero friends, unless you count the narrator of the book. Severin and the narrator are best friends. They smoke cigarettes at Severin's estate. They talk about literature, domestic violence, and the figure of the cruel woman. The cruel woman ambles roughshod over the grasses in the artworks of wealthy heterosexuals of European descent. Severin confesses to the narrator that one time he used science to bring the cruel woman to life. Like the wife in the blockbuster film *Bride of Frankenstein* (1935), the cruel woman was ill suited for love.

For example, the cruel woman chains Severin to a thick wooden rod. Then she orders a man of Greek descent to engage Severin's body in a whipping without Severin's consent. In addition, she breaks up with Severin while his body is still attached to the thick wooden rod. She refuses to have penetrative sex with Severin. No, they never have penetrative sex. The absence of penetrative sex is demoralizing to Severin, and yet it helps him to develop a political orientation, which positions him favorably on the job market.

I will elaborate.

"What doesn't kill you births a more virulent strain of your kind," writes Friedrich Wilhelm Nietzsche. Nietzsche is a German bachelor who rejects the companionship of people, preferring an assortment of handheld fireworks and domestic tools, such as sparklers and a hammer. He is famous for his virginal mustache. You aren't allowed to touch it!

Oh, Nietzsche.

While Severin is attached to the thick wooden rod, he is overwhelmed and close to death on account of the man of Greek descent who is whipping his body. Fast-forward a few days, and Severin is on holiday in Rome, tapping the virtues of socioeconomic status to process the traumatic romantic experience. In short, Severin endures. He perseveres like Queen Mab and pushes the hazelnut carriage of day laborers through the harrowing tunnel of the absence of maidenhood, dipping into the family coffers to buy himself a ration of the most exquisite cocaine. Later, in the heat of an Italian nightclub, Severin snatches a neon glowstick from a lesbian! Then he is dancing. Severin dances to express his sense of humiliation and loss. It isn't long before Severin's dancing draws the attention of a well-connected group. In a quiet velvet corner, nestled in the rear of the nightclub, the group plies Severin with liquor and a flight of hens stuffed with surprising flavor combos like cheese and nuts. Severin swears the group to secrecy. Then he shows them the blueprints for organizing society along strict hierarchical lines. They decide to get brunch after. The morning is dewy and bright, veined with silver torrents. It's beautiful! My god. It's beautiful. Severin is crying now. He is slobbering. He's choking a little. It's just so. Beautiful. He commits right then and there to join the fight for men's rights. In due time, he inherits his father's estate. That's how Severin evolves into the political persona we know and love today.

Severin owns classical paintings. Severin owns important books. Severin owns top-quality cigarettes. There's also a silk-clad thingy, plump in a bodice, walking on stilted doe's legs through the corridors of Severin's estate. The silk-clad thingy carries a platter of boiled eggs and meats.

As previously noted, Severin is an active participant in the men's rights movement. The author uses plain language to communicate Severin's identification with the figure of the tyrant. For these reasons and others, the naïve or hasty reader might be tempted to conclude, "Well, there you have it! Severin's a tyrant. This is a tyrannical novel!" To that reader, I would say, "Hold on. Slow down. The complexity of the text threatens otherwise."

For example, when the silk-clad thingy presents the platter of boiled eggs and meats, Severin reacts in an unexpected manner. He is overcome by anguish because the eggs are not cooked to his liking. The eggs have been hard-boiled, but Severin prefers soft-boiled eggs. His preference for the soft-boiled egg subverts the logic of tyranny.

I will elaborate.

Throughout the history of the West, tyrants have preferred to associate themselves with hard objects. Since there is no reason to assume this preference does not extend to eggs, the reader speculates that it is the natural tendency of the tyrant to choose the hard-boiled egg over the soft-boiled egg. If Severin were actually a tyrant, then he would have welcomed the hard-boiled egg into the sensitive inner-mouth space of his head. Severin does not welcome the hard-boiled egg into the sensitive inner-mouth space of his head.

The author of the novel outfits Severin's sensitive inner space with the trappings of a bachelor's boudoir. The boudoir is lined from floor to ceiling in the richest pink velvet. Ever since reading the book, I have caught myself salivating at the thought of spending the afternoon in Severin's mouth. One day, in the future, after I've put in my time and ascended some of the rungs, I hope to spend an entire weekend. I'll bring along a novel, plus several of my colleagues and friends! We'll discourse on literature, ethics, and the necessary exclusion of some groups from the public sphere. Incapable of preventing ourselves from caressing the walls, we'll wipe our fingers on the pink velvet surface. Then the room will begin to vibrate, and a deep-throated purring will fill up our ears.

In addition, and it goes without saying, the tyrant's preference for the hardness of hard-boiled eggs, and for hard objects in general, evokes the turgidity of the phallus when it is erect. This thrilling detail connects to a common misconception held by tyrants the world over: the disavowal of castration. The tyrant does not understand that he is castrated, but what about Severin? Does Severin understand that he is castrated? Yes, Severin understands that he is castrated. For example, before Severin realizes he must develop a method for training women to prevent women from hanging him, he takes orders from a woman. Severin is not your typical tyrant. He's a good person.

Granted, this is a complicated novel, due to the fascist overtones. Severin openly lays claim to tyranny. Severin supports his claim to tyranny via action—in one scene, for example, Severin threatens the silk-clad thingy with domestic violence because the eggs have not been cooked to his liking—but everybody knows that in the olden days Europe was unseemly. The sovereign put people to death. He didn't understand that he was castrated. Before casting judgement, I ask that you consider the following. Has Severin ever tried to conceal his unsavory political commitments from the reader? No, Severin has not. In fact, Severin has always been incredibly open and honest about the most troubling facets of his personality. His forthrightness is commendable in and of itself.

In return, we owe Severin a similar debt of honesty.

Let us strive to be honest. It feels good to be honest.

+ x +

Honestly, my memories of Severin are grim. I didn't like him. We met as graduate students in a middling creative writing program out west. The school no longer exists. It was cheaply affixed to the side of a mountain. Weakened by drought and fire, it eventually succumbed to gravity and was quietly shed like a scab. Nobody noticed it was gone.

Severin was a terrible writer and an emotionally manipulative personality. High on philosophy and art, he could reorganize the world by glancing at it. I remember how much it hurt to get caught up in his line of sight. I had to go and lie down. If I accidentally sat across from him in a seminar or workshop, then I'd be knocked out for days. "Influenza," I would say. I was always saying that. I couldn't stand him, and yet we were friends. That's how friendship worked in school. Then it was over. Severin and I fell out of touch. The school fell off the mountain. Yeah, I've thought about reaching out. I want to tell him I despise him. I want him to know that the whole time we were friends, I was despising him. The truth is, and I know this now, I despised myself. I despised the sight of me, and he never allowed me to turn away. He never allowed me to turn away, so I was in tremendous pain, pretty much all of the time. I was a person caught in the throes of pain. I'm not like that anymore. I've matured. I've learned to empathize with Severin's point of view. I've even incorporated his publications into my teaching and scholarship. I've tapped his novel like a keg and funneled its life force straight into my career. Thank you, Severin, for giving life to my career!

Okay. To be honest. To be totally and completely honest. There was a time in my life when I thought we'd be friends. Real friends. What happened was he caught me in the act. Past midnight. Starry sky. Dark, dry air. Cold. Out West. High up on the side of a mountain. In the center of campus, on the lawn of the admissions building, there's a statue of a beautiful woman ringed by evergreens. She's one of the wives of the founder of the state religion, the first wife or the main wife, and I'd wrapped her, beautiful statue, head to toe, in toilet paper that I stole from the student union.

You've got to understand. I've always been drawn to the wife in *Bride of Frankenstein* before she's opened, when her body and her head and her face are encased in gauze.

Yeah. So. I wrapped the statue of the founder of the state religion's wife in toilet paper. Then I was, you know, worshipping her. I was waiting. Waiting to see what's underneath. I pressed my face against the paper covering her skirt. Show me. That's when Severin intruded, his arms full of furs.

"You like statues," he said.

"I do."

"You wrap them in toilet paper."

"Yes."

"That's queer."

"Yes."

"You're queer."

"Yes."

"I like statues, too," he said. "I drape them in furs."

"I see. You're also queer?"

"I am."

"Good. That's good."

"We must stick together," he said.

"Okay."

He took me back to his place.

It was kind of a shitty place. There were roommates. Everywhere. But whatever, they were already asleep. There were some cats, too. I don't like cats. It's okay. Severin and I worked out a plan. First, we'd both take off our clothes. Next, I'd drape myself in furs and Severin would wrap himself in toilet paper. Then we'd just, I don't know, see what happened. We had a six-pack. A six-pack. He had some cigarettes. I like cigarettes. So let's see. We'll just wait and see. Where the night takes us.

Severin handed me an ermine stole and a sheepskin muff. He pushed me into the bathroom. Closed the door. I was alone. Bathroom was a little shitty. No. Yes. Shit streaking the seat of the toilet. Shit rimming the tub. Shit on the mirror. Shit staining the grout of the tile. Hairs collecting along a streak of shit, poking right up to God like asparagus. Okay. Here I am. What is a stole and what is a muff?

I know what I look like. I've looked plenty of times. It's fine. Someone should look like this. Someone should've looked like this. What the fuck. Do you want to know what a person looks like when they're wearing a stole and a muff? I already told you. I despised the sight.

I got low.

Then I got low. I was sitting on the floor, like Barbie. Legs straight out, what do they want? My attention? No, I don't want to hold them.

Severin was talking. He was explaining how to care for his cats.

What?

His cats. He told me to watch his cats. Over Christmas break. Hello, keep up.

Pay attention.

"Give them food and water," he said. "More importantly, get to know them. Spend time with them. That's crucial. Forget to feed them, and they'll survive. Forget to touch them? They'll fucking die."

That can't be right.

Okay. This is Severin's bedroom. The window is frosty. Frost is beautiful. Frost is beautiful. I need to throw up. I needed to throw up. Christmas gifts, everywhere. Severin had been shopping. Now he was taking his time. Packing a bag. He was going to miss his flight. Then there was that cat at my feet, roosting on an open magazine. Pink. It was pink. I didn't know you could get them that way.

"Which one is sick? Deleuze?"

I didn't say that. Please. I didn't say it. Is that what he calls his cat? I shouldn't have come here. I should never have come. I needed to throw up. I needed to throw up. I needed to. I had a knife. Okay, I had a knife. I had a knife. I hated when thinking happened like this and I could see myself on the outside. I hated that.

She was holding the knife and then, I see, she cut a gash in her throat. She stood over the cat, the pink cat, just to bleed on it for a minute. She bled on it? Yeah, she bled on it. Soon she was gonna drop. She was gonna drop. She was gonna drop. Don't let her drop on the cat. It was pink, the cat. But why was it pink?

I don't know!

Staggered. She staggered. She darted for the bookcase. She was looking for the book he liked the best. Which book did he like the best? The one where they slander the trees. They hated trees, Deleuze and Guattari. Assholes. She tore a page from the book and fed the crumpled blossom to the gash in her neck. She didn't throw up. I never threw up. It's like I didn't get how to do it. Do you understand?

Talking. Severin was talking. He said the cats aren't called Deleuze and Guattari, not anymore. He renamed them. He renamed his cats. He was always doing shit like that. Giving cats new names.

"Why?"

Severin shrugged. He sat down on the edge of the bed, crossed one leg over the other. What was he wearing. Indoor soccer shoes? I want a pair. I wanted a pair.

"Point to the one that gets the medicine," I said.

"The pink one gets medicine," he said.

The pink one? No.

No, no, no.

"No."

"What do you mean, no?"

I mean, who has a pink cat? I mean, "No."

No, no, no, no.

"Look," said Severin, and then he was up again, orbiting the bedroom. He was collecting the Christmas gifts in a gigantic paper bag. "It's been a long day. I shopped. I wrapped. I packed. I'm about to fly across the country." He stopped at the foot of the bed, hoisted a duffel over his shoulder. "Now I need to explain the concept of a joke to you?"

She couldn't get a read on his face. I couldn't see it either.

The sky was a snake. It sloughed off the skin of the sun.

Dark. It was dark.

+ x +

Now for a review of the literature. Some people argue that this novel is a transgressive novel because it features Severin. Severin is a castrated member of the ruling class and an aspiring poet with an impossible desire for submission. Other people argue that this novel is a subversive novel because it features Severin. Severin is a castrated member of the economic elite and an aspiring poet with a paradoxical dream to end capitalism. Plus, there are several persuasive arguments that say the novel is a queer novel, due to the superabundance of fur garments, which are gay.

My take on the situation is radical. I believe it is wrong to argue about books. Even though I spend Christmases with conservative colleagues and keep in touch with an elderly mentor who subscribes to the impossible dream of a white ethnostate, I believe that each and every member of the department is free to choose a literary heritage. I choose to join in the struggle to preserve the rights of the most important books of European civilization.

Ever since the dawn of the birth of the French person Roland Barthes, we have understood the college classroom to be an amphitheater for bearing witness to pleasure. Barthes worked hard in the public sphere to devise a repertoire of gestures for testifying to pleasure without explicating the text. He managed to conduct his life's work in silence. Total silence. It was important that Barthes stay quiet. He didn't want to spook the jouissance. The jouissance is skittish. It darts like a doe into berry bushes. Sometimes, at school, we coax the doe to the center of our circle. Thanks to Barthes's hard work, we've developed a ceremony for gathering round, opening our books, and pointing at pleasures that can neither be described nor verified. What does it mean? I will tell you what it means. It means the unspeakable quality of our pedagogy is the condition for a radical, intellectual faith. Studies have shown that TAs of faith lead healthier, happier, more integrated lives. They're able to make do on their stipends, with a little something leftover for the weekend. They outperform their peers on the job market. When they use their bodies to compose the formation of the sacred circle at school, the pleasure touches friends touching books listed on the syllabus, reinforcing the mission of the university.

High up. The sky is a snake.

It sloughs off the skin of the sun.

Dark. It's dark.

Somewhere in the once-vibrant city of Chernobyl, the snow is falling. We must be careful, vigilant, and tender because there are scholars who set traps in the snow and the berry bushes.

They aren't really scholars.

They aren't even readers.

They are fur traders whose thighs rub snaggles into off-brand stockings! Ambling roughshod over mass graves of frost-bitten grasses! Spooking the pleasure, which leaps like a doe, to impale its soft, soft self on the crystalline edges of the berry branches—dead!

She's dead.

Dead. Dead. Dead.

Severin lights a cigarette. The narrator lights a cigarette. The narrator peruses Severin's collection of animal skeletons, military hardware, and plastic cats.

According to the details of his biography, Severin belongs to the ruling class. But what about the narrator? Who is the narrator of the book?

The narrator's status is ambiguous. He employs a valet to grab hold of his arm whilst he is sleeping. The valet whispers the word "Hegel" into the narrator's ears. The intimacy of the gesture suggests that these two men are cut from similar cloths. If they are not, then we are definitely dealing with a class-traitor situation, which is incredibly thrilling and admirable.

The narrator and his valet are not biological brothers, yet they manage to coexist in a quivering jelly dome called brotherhood. Therefore, structurally, the narrator and his valet are brothers. They are brothers.

Let us pan out.

Severin, the narrator, the valet, and the reader each occupy different positions along the socioeconomic spectrum. Despite these unfortunate material circumstances, each one has uploaded himself into the exact same tradition of arts and letters, which garners harsh jeers from the members of the older generations. But is it not true that the most important books disrupt the laws of bourgeois decorum?

Severin laughs. He lights the cigarette.

The narrator laughs. He lights the cigarette.

When the silk-clad thingy presents the platter of boiled eggs and meats, Severin discovers that the eggs have not been cooked to his liking. He subjects the silk-clad thingy to the threat of domestic violence. The silk-clad thingy flees like a freaked robot on bent doe's legs. That's the cue for Severin and the narrator to continue their conversation.

Okay. No more pretense. We are friends, yes?

Then allow me to touch you where you need to be touched.

You are a person deserving of your life.

I'll say it again. You are a person deserving of your life.

There was once something sharp and damnable residing in the folds of your personhood, but it's been lovingly rewritten or redacted at school. Wish it well. Let it go. Today is the day you submit your dissertation.

You're doing what's right, seeking gainful employment. It goes without saying that you've suffered. The suffering was real. It helped you develop a political orientation, which will grant you a favorable position on the job market. I will elaborate.

You haven't hurt anyone.

You haven't hurt anyone.

You have wanted, and your wanting makes you precious, but you have not taken what you want by force. You haven't hurt anyone.

You are a peach.

You're a lamb moseying home on pointy little feet!

Munching clovers.

Moving slowly.

You can afford to move slowly.

Because it feels good to be you.

You're homely and hospitable.

You're inhabitable.

You feel good.

You feel so good.

This feels good.

Come. Now is the time to act. Let us not look back on this day and wonder why our eyes were content to be separated, stuck in their own jellied heads. Lonely.

This feels so good.

Forging thicker bonds.

Building better bodies for whispering the word "Hegel."

For sharing the word "Hegel."

Whilst sleeping.

Don't worry, you haven't forgotten how to sleep.

You're sleeping now.

The sky is a snake.

It sloughs off the skin of the sun.

Dark.

The way is dark.

Dry air.

High up.

Ringed by evergreens.

Quiet.

Be quiet.

Come to us on your hands.

Use your fingers to find it.

The pinhole, the puncture.

Gracing the skin of the birthday balloon.

That rides on the night of the sky tucked deep deep inside, deep inside the fold of your little lonely little lonely life.

Let it go.

The screaming is the sound of the starter.

On its cue. On its cue.

Let us.

Let us let us let us shed our flesh and shed our flesh and and and pool our resources.

Sacrament

Q. What is it?

A. It is a character in a novel at a hotel in France. It is seated on the bed, which is scarlet. It is thrown onto its back!

Q. Who is he?

A. He is English. He stands over the bed. He's having a good look at it.

Q. He takes a "good" look at it. If you dress the term in quotations, then the reader is better alerted to the undecidability. For example, one may ask, for one has every right to do so, is his gaze kindly or prurient, i.e., good or "good"? How do you think it will answer?

A. "The paraphraser is *so* artistic," writes Friedrich Wilhelm Nietzsche, a German opera queen. Nietzsche explains, "To paraphrase is to perform one's best impression of it, whether it is in mortal danger or not." If I were asked to perform my best impression of it, then I would say, "Good god, British rapscallion! Avert ye eyes from me lap where there she sits, me downstairs-heart, for she knows not yet the harsh sting of comic villainy!" It is a virgin.

Q. But it is French. Do they do it differently in France?

A. In that case, it answers, "L'homme est gentil." It is French. The rapscallion is English. He speaks in a style that causes me nausea and terror. In addition, I would not call him "good-looking." However, it is a fact that he is somewhat well off, which helps. For example, he has hired a French valet called Flowers?? Due to his position in society, the rapscallion is allowed to ignore the repellent aspects of his person. Mainly, his head and his face. They don't make humans like him anymore. Nowadays, the people are split right up the middle on the inside, too.

Q. Who?

A. Literature. Plus, the rapscallion's hair is blond and choked by a ribbon. It's a lot like Gertie's hair. Gertie is a character in the blockbuster film *E. T. the Extra-Terrestrial* (1982). The ribbon in the rapscallion's hair is blue. The hairstyle is appropriate for the time and place, but the idea of the ribbon intimately holding hairs like a bride's stinking bouquet from hell may be uncomfortable for some readers to picture. Whether it is possible for the reader to close the mind's eye, repressing the image of the rapscallion's head and hairs, is a question that falls beyond the scope of this conversation. In *E. T. the Extra-Terrestrial*, for example, Gertie is unattractive and slow witted. I don't know if her negative qualities stem from her hair, but let's just say that her hair isn't helping—

Q. Helping what?

A. The action to rise. The rapscallion's cheeks are scarlet, just like the bedspread on the bed he is circling, slowly and majestically, like a tampon-headed eagle.

Q. What happens next?

A. It is difficult to say because the identity of the object is lacking in clarity.

Q. Is the object an organ? Or is it a purse with a coin shoved inside?

A. "It constitutes an economy of the undecidable," writes Jacques Derrida, a French televangelist. "It is not dialectical but plays with the dialectic." Derrida describes the playfulness of the economy as an event of hysterical mourning squished between the twin pillars of Hegel-grief (which grows love, binding the brothers) and something that corresponds to the shape of a dildo that belonged to a gay person's mother. Derrida explains the undecidable economy through the figure of a clown inside a barn who is showing the audience how he raped it and married it and

murdered it by turns. (For an approximate visual representation of the ~~crime~~, see Figure 1.) As the Brothers Grimm
were wont to say, this is the moment when sorrow ends
and ~~joy~~ begins.

Q.   But does it have sex with him? Or are they just making love
by sentiments? In other words, is it taken by force? Or is it
fairly (i.e., tenderly) purchased by the rapscallion?

A.   Exactly. Next, the rapscallion goes outside and stands by
the hotel gate. It beats me as to whether he is enjoying a
cigarette or a cigar or a joint because the narrative doesn't
capture those kinds of details. If it were up to me, then he
would be enjoying a cigarette because smoking a cigarette
by the gate of a hotel is one of life's greatest pleasures! The
rapscallion stands by the gate and watches a parade of men
strut by atop several gorgeous fingers and toes. They wade
through a web of the kindest nature. The kindest nature
is like a Mother Nature figure, but instead of taking the
form of a plain Jane, which is sweet faced but can be short
with gentlemen—and they don't like to be reminded of
what is pushed forth from her nethers—she mimics an
immaculate-virgin type of gal. She's just really open and
forgiving and has curly hair with green leaves all over it. As
the rapscallion is experiencing this organic ecstasy of the
kindest nature, he is becoming charitably connected to the
other men in the vicinity. He is especially moved by one
who is a beggar, which is incredibly human and touching.
The economy was not good back then for the poor. The
economy is not good for the poor and the educated today.
But we've been swallowed up by a totally different kind

of episteme. Therefore, it is impossible and irresponsible to say anything further on the plight of the poor and the educated. The beggar whispers lewdly into the ear of a dame, or so it would seem. Later, the author explains how the beggar manipulates ladies using flattery so they will be moved to pay him coins—

Q. And then?

A. The rapscallion takes off for a grand walk through the beauteous French countryside!

Q. Why?

A. He's looking for something. He's on the hunt for something sad. The countryside is mostly yellow sun, gray fog, families with valets that don't require harsh treatment, and lots of grasses. That's where the rapscallion finds it! It's in the grasses! In a ditch! It takes him by surprise.

Q. What is it?

A. It's the word for ungenius. No, it's something not reading. Or it's a body dumbly breathing, growing its hair, filling its fat. Don't put the thought in its head. Round the plush fork of its thighs. It reclines on its side. On a chaise? Some grass? Its hair and the grass make a species, are familiars. Exquisite crops: a texture. Massages the palms of his hands. Green blade. Green blade. Green blade. Extravagant separation. Its hair. The grass. Edges the ignorance. Fork of its fat. He cries out at the sight of it. "Aaaaah-ha-ha-ha-ha-ha-ha-ha!" The cry rips a hole in his heart. Then he moves on. Off again, off again. Passing barns and broth-els like an anthropomorphic engine. He chugs up a can-dy-cane hill and sings to himself. "I—am—not—a—mas-ter—I—am—not—a—master!" Comes to the moment, comes to the point, the grand—

Figure 1: *"Perpetual, the rape."*

You Hated Yourself?

If they're reading, then they're growing. Then they hardly are paid. They live with friends. The cheapest arrangement. A house. Near a tree. Upon a streak of ground. The campus. Shit on the sidewalk. On the lawn. On the stoop. Smudged on the lens of the sky.

Graduate students. Greg and Kyle and Micah and Jerome.

They walk home after lunching on the quad to hang a poster on the basement wall. The poster is famous and French. It's called Acéphale: the Headless Man. They bought it on Etsy. Acéphale is missing a head, and the grad students are sitting beneath him on the faded floral-print couch. There's a bong and some beers, a copy of something anxious by Blanchot. The scene is so perfect, it's practically fascist. But it isn't fascist.

I will elaborate.

Fascists once called for a return to values like these: communal living, anxious literature beneath the sign of man—but *with* a head! The presence of the head was nonnegotiable for the fascists. Fascists always included the head. Grad students prefer to have the head removed. There would seem to be a difference—

"That's what she said!" says Jerome.

Now Kyle is groaning. He flips the hair off his face. "Your timing is terrible."

"It's because he doesn't get it," says Greg.

"I do get it," says Jerome.

"Then prove it," says Greg.

"The difference," says Kyle.

"Is spreading," says Greg.

"Her thighs," says Micah.

Jerome is red, a valentine rose. "That's what Alice B. Toklas said!"

[GENERAL LAUGHTER]

Greg and Kyle and Micah and Jerome.

Acéphale.

Odd, really. The friends' strange poster does figure a head in the form of a skull, which is worn on the groin of the man with no head, except for the head that hangs on the groin in the shape of a skull. But does the skull count as a head? Who bore the skull when the body was alive? A virgin? Did the skull once sit on the living neck of a virgin? Acéphale, the headless man who wears a virgin's—see what I mean, the head isn't properly his, if it's even a head at all, categorically. Because it's a skull. That belonged to a virgin.

The logic won't hold.

The difference is spreading.

It's stretching the skin.

It happens like this. After seminar there are drinks. After drinks Greg says, "Do you want to go to the bedroom to—"

"Okay."

"—look at my father?"

He's talking about a photograph. He wants to show you a photograph. Of his father. There it is, tacked to the board above his desk. A black-and-white image. Small and grainy. It looks like shit.

"You know that feeling you get when you simultaneously loathe and absolutely respect a person?" Greg tugs the photo free and hands it to you. He closes his eyes. "It's more than a feeling," he continues. "It's a way of being in the world. It's like asking a question without expecting an answer because you prefer the ache of the open to the easy fascism of convention. No one gets what he wants. No one gets what he wants. You must never, never give me what I want. That's what I want. Now, if you'll forgive me this once for naively seeking the universal through the particularity of an eroticism, then I'll wager the following. You want it, too. Everyone does."

You're holding the photo, pressing your thumb on the face.

"I'm sorry," Greg says. "I'm still talking. Typical. There I go again, off on some tangent about the nature of desire." He smiles. "You're sweet, aren't you? You're, like, the opposite of judgmental."

Acéphale. Acéphale. Acéphale.

The Acéphale is vulnerable during seminar when nobody's home. No Greg. No Kyle. No Micah. No Jerome. You want to ruin the poster, like weather. The rain. The opportunity presents itself via Greg. He hands you a copy of the key to the house. "In case I lose mine," he says.

"Then borrow Jerome's."

"Suppose he loses his, too?"

"Then borrow Micah's."

"Suppose he loses his, too."

"Then you'll call Kyle."

"Think about it," says Greg. He smiles. "There's so much to lose."

What is friendship?

You steal from Greg. You steal the photo of Greg's father. Faded, grainy, creased. It looks like shit. You tuck it in the elastic band of your underwear.

What are you?

Greg is talking. "My father was almost a priest." Greg laughs. "My father knew God was real, but his knowledge wasn't totalizing or anything." He smiles. "Once Dad was lounging on a chaise by the pool. Next to him there was another chaise, and it was totally empty. I mean, I'm talking about a painfully empty chaise. Unbearable. My father was overcome by a feeling of certainty. In a moment he knew God wasn't there. It's a difficult thing to explain. Okay, take Kierkegaard for example—"

"What did he say."

"I forget," says Greg. "Something to do with his girlfriend. She refused to forgive him, you know, which was simultaneously sexy and inhumane."

Greg overuses the word "simultaneously," which functions to irritate your person and prose. *Don Quixote* is simultaneously comic and tragic. The hymen is a ghostly veil which desire wants to love and murder, simultaneously. The novel attacks the body of the text and the body of woman, simultaneously. *Lolita* is simultaneously comic and tragic. "You are the night," writes Georges Bataille, simultaneously bleeding from his throat and violating the girl. The viewer simultaneously sees and is seen by René Magritte's blue-blue eye. Tender tycoon, what is the test of intelligence? The ability to hold two opposed ideas in the mind at the same time, and still retain the wherewithal to maintain arousal.

Who cares about the man from La Mancha?

The mantis-shaped man looms up and over the law. Is lodged in a quivering jelly dome called fantasy.

Onward runs the thin, folded horse. Hooves swarm to a bunch. The punk's pink tongue tests the sheet of bubblegum. Stretches the skin. Enters the world. Like rain. It will rain.

Silly man.

Barber's basin.

Rain.

Fuck.

Silly basin. Headless man. Yells with a tongue bent out. Wants to swell another man's heart.

The mantis-shaped man looms up and over the library. Massages the mood. Like weather. Stretches the skin.

Fuck.

There's the bit about a sassy pupil and a childlike master. One says, "The time has come, dear friend, for your genius to flee like a whore from the burning brothel of your body." The other closes his eyes, accepts finitude. The failure grows love, binding the brothers.

Greg and Kyle and Micah and Jerome.

The campus, all of it.

The quad.

That grass. The town and the farms. Those stupid fucking barns.

One red pig.

The lily-white sheep.

Fuck it, there's some farmland. There's a field, crows all over it. Those little oily pies. Beak ends tucked up in the husks, smeared on the organs, smeared on the seeds that rest in the belly of the man who is pierced by a rod. Sun's out. Lovely like that in the harvest.

Hardworking.

Farmers are friends, fathers, and brothers, plus the one who is pierced by a thick wooden rod. The one who is staked to the ground, crazed as a crucifixion, nine hours in. Dancing on a stick, he's spilling hay. He's spilling oils. He's shedding crows like obsidian balloons snipped free from the taught intestinal strings. Swollen airborne bundles.

You want to make something pop.

The maniac man is staked to the ground, deep in a field of tall white wheat. He calls out, a weaker Jesus, and says he's a knight. "I'm a knight! I'm a knight!" He says he's in love with a woman. He really believes that he loves her, a woman. Fuck him. Fuck him. You will murder his horse.

One red pig or the lily-white sheep.

Campus.

You could be inside it.

The dingiest corner of the campus café. The place that holds sex like the weather. There at the roundest, stickiest table some grad students are studying the history of the novel.

Once there was a person in a novel who willingly abdicated his purchase on totality. This produced a political revolution called "the supreme spasm of infinite masturbation." Years later, a person in a novel was minding his business, fingering the crack in a tasteless piece of handmade pottery: a metaphor for the structural instability of the text. Then came a figure for the author of the book. He lived in a novel. Very transgressive—

The grad students are kissing and crying because they are moved by the intimacy of reading. They decide to share a mammoth piece of blueberry coffee cake. There they go, poking their forks at the crumbling body like concerned citizens sifting through the remains of a decimated brothel.

"What happened?"

"Who knows."

"Any survivors?"

"What do you care."

"What does your mother care? I fucked her right here last night."

"Mama, no!"

[GENERAL LAUGHTER]

The students compile their notes.

The long-standing deep nature of these ties this trusting friendship unfailing friendship intelligence rigor strict sense of academic responsibility the difficulty is always to distinguish between on the one hand a sexual violence that is tolerable in a way because it is structural the violence which inhabits relations of passion and love devotion and goodwill profoundly touches profoundly touches the worthiness of our university unfailing friendship work devotion and goodwill a fine spirit of cooperation justice attachment to the university this trusting friendship pleasure respect gratitude neither any coercion or violence nor any attack on the presumed "innocence" of a twenty-seven- or twenty-eight-year-old adult where does she find the grounds devotion and goodwill how can she claim to have the right to initiate such a serious procedure with pleasure with all the friendship intelligence rigor integrity the future and the reputation bear witness worthiness of our university unfailing friendship at work at work worked for so long so long with pleasure respect with pleasure and gratitude with all the friendship the friendship and devotion.*

The students are buoyant with relief. They were fearing they'd uncover evidence of a violence beyond the limit of the tolerable.

"Gender is like a frontispiece but metaphysical," says Greg.

Greg closes his eyes.

He smiles.

"Faith is intelligence," Greg says. "My father knew God wasn't there. He knew it. He was so young then, too. twenty or twenty-five. He was better looking than I am. Well, this photo, the quality is terrible, so maybe it's hard to tell—"

Tell him. "You're ashamed of your father."

---

* Jacques Derrida, "Letter from Jacques Derrida to Ralph J. Cicerone, then Chancellor of UCI," July 25, 2004, Jacques Derrida, accessed December 9, 2017, http: www.jacques-derrida.org/Cicerone.html and "Politics of Difference," in For What Tomorrow ... A Dialogue (Stanford: Stanford UP, 2004).

"I don't want to become my father. As a human being, sure, okay, he's problematic. He almost became a priest. He's from a different time."

"He's an imbecile."

"Actually? He's an extremely ethical person. Do you even want to get to know me? I mean, don't you want to—"

"No."

"Look, I've got a little brother, too," he says. "Of course, the relationship between brothers is," Greg whistles. "Well, it's huge." He laughs. "People who aren't brothers, they just can't comprehend. Brothers are forced to enjoy farcical wandering, much like Don Quixote, which is almost sexual. Well, okay, it is sexual. That's what's so intense. But Dad didn't have a brother. He had one in a literal sense. A literal sense, or maybe a biological sense, sure. But metaphorically? He was metaphorically bereft. He was aesthetically—"

From here the sun really does resemble a baby pervert. But bigger. Bigger. Cherubically bloated. Fucking sick. But it's true. He's real. Rotten sun, up at the top. Soft and round. Watches things clogging the countryside, all that the barns can't contain. This lyrical land with some shitty debris!

Four p.m. The yellow-fucking disc jerks himself down. Casting shadows on dumb objects. Shading the corn, the wheat, the dust on the boots. The farmers are working in the fields, and then there's the Quixote staked to the earth like the shit son of a crucified God. Everything reeks. Human shit is mixed in with the shit of the cows. Human shit is stuck to the soles of the boots, flecked on the laces.

Flecked on the toe.

The big toe.

The big toe and the language of flowers. The big toe and the language of flowers. Mouth. Inner experience. Mouth. Sovereignty. Mouth. The solar anus. Sacred world. The notion of expenditure. The meaning of the general economy. Rotten sun. Rotten sun and the lugubrious game—

"Aaaaah-ha-ha-ha-ha-ha-ha-ha." The farmers are coming in the fields.

You must kill Quixote's horse.

Poison it (hand-feed it poison). Then ride it to the edge of a cliff. Shit in the wind. Rotting, shit-stained sky. Slide yourself from the horse to the ground. Keep the photo of his father in place, pinned to your skin by the elastic waist of your underwear. When your feet touch dirt, throw your weight.

A straight switch or a stick.

The rod.

The scepter, a stick, or the rod.

Some wickerwork. What is wickerwork?

Fuck.

On campus the night is pitch and you are a vomiting star. You are a poor and puking little thing. Are you twinkling? Did you lose your phone? Check the pocket of your jeans.

Don't fucking touch me.

He will find you on campus, the lovely man from La Mancha. He hides on the face of the creep in the corn. His head is lodged in the break of the day, his life held fast by the cleft of the tree. Even the dew becomes him, a measure of idiocy to slicken the air.

Campus.

What the fuck is a campus?

The photo, your underwear.

A bundle of twigs for flogging.

A scepter or stick.

A scepter, a stick, or the rod.

What, a shoot from some shitty willow?

Fuck.

is only in touch
with the soul via the body.

The Strange Case of the Yale School:
How to Review a Movie

Summarize the movie in one provocative yet informative phrase.

A found-footage occult-horror flick in which the waning relevance of post-structuralist theory drives aging comp-lit professors to Faustian extremes.

Identify the setting, premise, and central characters. Say what happens.

The year is 2016. The scene opens onto a windowless boardroom located on a college campus in the heart of Manhattan. The principal characters comprise a panel of accomplished scholars. They sit in the configuration of a line at the front of the room, holding pain in the puckers of their mouths and shouldering the onslaught of a stagnant yellow gloaming. The gloaming pools on the surfaces and soaks the textiles, fleshy pads, and synthetic grasses. The audience is gathered in cheap folding chairs edging the buffet table. The viewer knows the audience members by the backs of their heads, only the backs of their heads. The director's savvy decision to withhold the faces imparts an anonymous, bureaucratic flavor to the scene. Plus, there are many different hairs that grow on the heads, establishing an avant-garde color palette and contributing a whimsical texture to the grassland, which is cardboard. Long ago, the prairie was stenciled and cut. Now it grows into the startled shape of an indigo blazer.

Scholar One commences the séance by invoking the muses and thanking the women professors for teaching post-structuralist theory in the '80s. "I was assigned a reading list that constitutes the entire canon of the trinity," he says. "It was heavily centered in the French tradition—and this was pre-resistance! I just absorbed."[1]

The '80s were the salad days of Scholar One. In the '90s, as a graduate student, he experienced a period of hardship because the texts of Paul de Man were banned from the public sphere. Like true-blue persons of Jewish descent did starlight circumcisions to blow off Hellenization, he worked hard to keep the theory alive for future generations. Cramming himself onto a private perch in a secret society, he read the texts of the late Paul de Man.

I identify with Scholar One when he discusses the extreme experience of having to go into hiding so you can do all your reading in private. "We kind of read all these things under the table, in secret

---

1 "Theory at Yale: The Strange Case of Deconstruction in America." YouTube, uploaded by the NYU Center for the Humanities, 10 March 2016, https://www.youtube.com/watch?v=rSZw_EWojEY

and silence. We read and discussed every single text by Paul de Man, but outside of seminar."[2]

The grasses bloomed and wasted, wasted and bloomed, and eventually it was no longer the '90s. Meanwhile, Scholar #3 takes his right hand and places it on his own throat, digging into a soft bubble. His visage is troubled, like the sun has set behind the frontier of his face. His outlook contributes pathos to the scenery, underscoring the serious nature of going into hiding.

The movie is skilled at inserting new chapters into the lifeblood of acclaimed scholar Paul de Man. At first, de Man appears as an everyman figure who works hard in the public sphere to ascend some of the rungs. Sooner or later, de Man gains enough altitude to find employment in a holy-trinity configuration at Yale. In addition to becoming one portion of a Christian god, the movie reveals how de Man was also a patron of the fairer sex because during his lifetime he labored to make spaces for sliding women into the bulkhead of the university. Then the boat sank. Scholar One recites the names of everyone who died in the wreckage. "I mention these women because they saw that deconstruction was actually an opening," he says, "and not something that closed down discourse in a kind of boys' club."[3]

I'd never heard the touching stories of these women before, which is why I'm glad I decided to watch the movie. In addition, there's an aura of mystery that surrounds the aftermath of the shipwreck.

---

2 *Ibid.*
3 *Ibid.*

The director was blessed with immense luck when he did the casting. He got the only survivor of the wreckage to be in the movie. The survivor perches on the panel with the scholars to "represent the experiential aspect of things."[4] A long time ago, she explains, she enrolled in a seminar taught by the late great Paul de Man. Back then, she was no more than "a naïve graduate student."[5] In fact, it was her naïveté that inspired her to drop Paul de Man's seminar after the first day of class. That's why she wasn't on board when the boat hit the iceberg. "It was clearly one of the great mistakes of my career," she says.[6] I am deeply saddened for her loss, and yet I see the truth in it. Her career has suffered greatly. I'd never even heard of her before watching the movie.

The Second Scholar's presentation is a chastening of the punks who scribbled obscenities onto a defenseless photograph of Paul de Man, publishing it in the *Chronicle of Higher Education*. "The people gave de Man a face only to deface it in a violent act because de Man turned out to be a terrible person."[7] The scholars in the movie hold defacement to be the shallowest of humanistic offenses. It's obvious to everybody on the panel. Those scribbling punks at the *Chronicle* were beholden to humanism, which is the *exact* thing de Man worked tirelessly to eliminate in the public sphere.

Scholar #3 continues to choke himself, digging a thumb into the bubble of his neck. He admits to having once glimpsed his own "little face in the book, which was really quite disturbing."[8] I can

---

4 *Ibid.*
5 *Ibid.*
6 *Ibid.*
7 *Ibid.*
8 *Ibid.*

see how that could be a disturbing experience for a certain kind of person. It's like, all those times you thought you were reading? You were looking at a mirror. Scholar #3 persisted through the disturbance, which is admirable and endearing. Moving on, he teaches the viewer many thrilling details about translation, collaboration, and deconstruction. The best part of the presentation is when he tells a story about the time he collaborated with a dead homosexual to translate Paul de Man into Spanish.

When you're collaborating with another translator you are in some kind of strangely erotic fratricidal battle. And you're in that same kind of erotic fratricidal battle with the author whose work you're translating. That seems to me to be indissociable from deconstruction. But that, I think, was not clear to us in the '80s and '90s. It wasn't until recently that the articulation of deconstruction with the figure of translation has become uh much clearer. And uh the person with whom I was working to translate that book, a dear friend, now dead, was one of the first gay people that I worked with very, very closely. For me, it was an extraordinary opportunity to uh enter into a world, a relation, a set of possibilities that was allowed to me by the work of collaborative translation in a specific way that is fratricidal and erotic. It's a collaboration where you're working really, really hard late into the night over tremendously strong Puerto Rican coffee um to get something right about a text. And I can't think of a better way to talk about deconstruction or the Yale school than that. Really, really, really late-night coffee-laden fratricidal but also sort of eroticized translation sessions, uh. With that I'll leave you.[9]

His soul drops out through the bottom, and the spirit of Paul de Man assumes full possession of the corpus. The touching

---

9 *Ibid.*

relationship between scholar and ghost is reminiscent of the "supreme collaboration" between Henry Frankenstein and Doctor Septimus Pretorius in *Bride of Frankenstein* (1935).

"I've come home!" says Paul.

Really it's the ghost communicating through the body to make it enact Paul de Man's signature rapid hand gestures. In the movie, this is called "flipping my fingers."[10]

For a visual of "flipping my fingers," see Figures 1–6.

Describe the theme. Explicate the significance.

There are two major themes: sexual repression and spiritual possession. The themes battle for dominance in the movie, much like they've battled for dominance throughout the ages, within the global arenas of sexology and psychoanalysis.

The problem is classical. Is the patient repressing a portion of himself? Or is the patient possessing a body that he cannot recognize as his own? The solutions will vary, depending on your take on the mind-body question. IRL, analysts have tended to favor the theory of sexual repression. Tons of people suffer from it. But a movie isn't life because anything can happen in it. In this movie the theme of spiritual possession triumphs, producing a utopian vision of the world, society, friendship, and academia.

I will elaborate.

---

10 *Ibid.*

No doubt there are many viewers who would argue that Scholar #3 is repressed. He's repressed, plain and simple. He's just your average, run-of-the-mill repressed person. Because he wanted to get fucked by that homosexual friend he drank coffee with in Puerto Rico. Very common, especially within the ivory towers. To them I would say:

You're wrong. That's a lazy man's reading, no offense. It's lacking in both imagination and heart. Scholar #3 is not repressed. He's possessed. He's possessed by Paul de Man.

Just for argument's sake, let us consider that Scholar #3 is gay. That's fine. It's usually a good thing nowadays. I happen to be gay myself. But, more importantly, if Scholar #3 were gay, then wouldn't he probably want to be possessed by Paul de Man? Well, okay. In this movie he gets to be both. The director has managed to erect an acutely generous worldview. Everyone wins. ☺

The bald fact of spiritual possession allows us to imagine a universe in which haunting is a facet of daily life. This perspective might be old fashioned inside twenty-first century academia, but the truth is I wouldn't be able to live with myself if I didn't put it forth. To my mind, literary scholarship has not fully explored the possibilities of a haunted worldview.

Who wouldn't want to live in a haunted world? Look, I know there are many trendy ideas these days about monism, vibrant matter, and the like, et cetera. But who do you think enlivens the flesh?? Since watching the movie, I've come to understand that a human being is very complex. No matter the sex, gender, hairstyle, disability, citizenship status, race, or ethnic background, he is comprised of at least two entities: a body and a soul; and possibly more than one soul. If there should be bodies with multiple souls, then there's no reason why there couldn't also be soulless bodies and bodiless souls. In a world like the world of the movie, to exist as a disembodied soul would be scientifically and philosophically verifiable, and *totally normal* as well. This is why it is vitally important to increase everyone's access to governmental research grants, substantial housing vouchers, open border migration policies, universal basic income with health care included, inexpensive over-the-counter hormones, and public unisex bathhouses.

Now's the time to put the pieces together. Present a key moment or idea.

So the audience is in a nonstop swoon once the spirit of Paul de Man descends to take up residence in the body of Scholar #3. The narrative becomes bothered like the lurching forth of tumbleweeds. They roll along on the prairie just because it feels so good to them. In my opinion, the director allows the plot to run roughshod, but whether he is doing so on purpose or because of an honest lack of talent is not my place to judge. Only time will tell.

The audience becomes unruly like the unthinking masses who pool resources and murder the monster because they are incapable of understanding difference. This happens at night, and some of them are carrying torches. Using the body of Scholar #3, Paul de Man addresses the crowd, delivering a speech in the style of a coach before the game.

There are names that could be named of academics who acted in collaboration with the mediatized representation of deconstruction and theory. They collaborated to purge Yale by not granting tenure, by making life impossible. And those people are still with us. Some of them are retiring soon, we hope, but there was an active de-De Man-ization of the profession that was the acting out of this personifica-tion in the most vicious and reprehensible way. I don't think that we should tell the story without remembering the people who were the victims of it, and the damned perpetrators as well![11]

During the Q&A, a man in the mob cries out. He wants to bring them back. Who? The people purged from Yale, plus everyone who got killed in the shipwreck. The man throws his face to the heavens and screams at the panelists. "How do we bring them back?!"[12] Very touching.

Ever since *Bride of Frankenstein* (1935), it has been politically risky to advocate pressing the pieces of the dead into the services of life. The allusion to *Bride of Frankenstein* is a sign that the director is using the medium of film to think through complicated ethical questions con-cerning humans and nonhumans. By now the average viewer is probably perched on the edge of his seat, thinking:

They're going to bring them back. My god. They're going to bring them back. But how? How? How?! In Jesus's name, I hope they ar-en't planning to harness the power of reproductive science so as to assemble the pieces.

Perhaps it is due to my background and proclivities, but I am not the average viewer; for me, *Bride of Frankenstein* is acutely erotic due to the gauze that encases the head of the wife.

Evaluate the movie.

In the final days since watching the movie, I've thought a lot about the environment. Like, what was the taste of the prairie before the advent

---

11 *Ibid.*
12 *Ibid.*

of farmland? It is a misguided effect of humanism that the wasted plains which we recklessly call "the face" should even cohere at all before our eyes. I am reminded of my favorite song, "Personal Jesus." The singer advocates the viewer to reach out and touch face, and I for one have always harbored a clandestine desire to master the frontier that expands beyond the edges of a beautiful person with a beautiful body. There's so much we have yet to uncover on God's great green material planet. There must exist, for example, a rare form of joy to perfect what was joyless in everyone. Just last week, scientists discovered the opposite of a constellation. It's a demonic grail in the sky. Now it is possible to step outside for a walk in the navy blue night and drop off the edge of the homestead.

Figures 1-6: "Flipping my fingers."

Host

You wanted a father because of the memory you did not possess. The stories, others had them. Like the one in which a father is begotten, or the father vomits, or he is vomited.

[3] one of them says he won't do it.

[4] one rushes unseen.

[5] he fell over.

There's another one where he walks upright.

But what of the priest what priest? You lived in a town with a priest. That's a kind of father, so everything was okay for you. It wasn't you weren't satisfied. You went to confess. There were mounds along the way green, brown, or guts colored. Sometimes blood. When it was raining. The homes were wet like blood. A decomposing body in a fleshy shroud you had a way of hastily walking to the cathedral.

Sometimes you were satisfied. There were two of you. You stood in the cathedral. One and two. There was also a third. Where? The third kept to itself.

There were stories of crimes rapes and murders maybe this is one.

The cathedral was haunted.

There was a ghost he was a knight. The ghost? A suit of armor covering the arms. An iron helmet in the place of the head. And he wasn't wearing bottoms so people could see it a penis. But knew they the breadth of it?

Mass was impossible.

The knight loved to bark. Would bark with the priest beside the priest or behind. The knight loved to vibrate sometimes before beside and behind. The bottomless knight but knew they the breadth of it? The bottomless knight with stars a member in martial manner pitched that semicircled moon take it up ye who are hungry for prayer take it up! Eat. Eat it. The tainted sliver. Or I will wield it as a bleach-hooked horn through which to sprinkle your poisoned brains into the starry air!

Here there is nothing unusual. Here nothing is wrong. Everything's as common as blood. Half-boring like red. Spirits parade about naked because they believe themselves to be clothed in garments.

You had an imagination.

There were three holy shrouds black red and pink. The shrouds were oracles no the shrouds were mouths. Okay, they were both. You wore the black shroud to speak the mildness of your mind it said the people shall be spared. That means you are merciful. The red shroud signified slaughter indiscriminate inefficient what? Well not all of them will be slaughtered.

One day the priest came to your house which one? The first one but the second one was there too. The priest said you are possessed. What? He said we must hold an exorcism for you. Which one? I'll be the host you said. Technically it's the body, replied the priest. Have you the bread and the wine?

It's stale, you said. I'm sorry it's not like I've hosted a dinner before. This bread represents it my very first try.

The priest sat down at the dining table he sliced the bread with the knife he ate but what of you? What? Did you not feast? Were you so daintily brought up you'd refuse your own flesh?

But you were eating. You ate.

The snow jetty the pink shroud it meant death and hell for everyone the ghost too the knight. You see he was castrated by you he was castrated by you but he took a long time to die. It was boring almost. It was? No! There wasn't any blood left in him the game it was called waiting, and finally:

a red drop dripped from the severed limb [DRIP] and then the knight was dead! So was everyone else! You were dead, even you were dead! Even though you were loved? You were dead even though you had loved, yes. Yes. And the exorcism? When? Now!

Okay. [DING] The doorbell. It was the priest he was there to ex-
orcise you. Which one? You didn't answer.

On the couch, you were on the couch. You were occupied you were
occupied by you. So the priest let himself in, he stepped inside
Welcome and thank god you have come said the priest. But this
is my house! you said. It really was your house. [DING] The bell
again. Who was it now? It was the third.

Welcome said the priest. Come in. Come in.

The priest gathered you round. The priest said, Look at thy father.
That's me. I'm that father from the story the one where he marched
with the host round the earth I put out wars with a dove I poked at
the earth with my sword the earth cleaved in twain then the host and
I we hopped into the hole we descended that dreary vault to smack
the fatal sisters and to pull on their hairs because they were out of
control! They were totally on their own down there in the dank. Had
they guidance? No! Then they must have had strictures. No nor had
they light and where there was only the night I raised up the moon
for my flag I sprinkled stardust on it and then 'twas twilight, all twilight I cuddled with a fallen female and fed it ambrosia to show how
I am not the one to say whose lips are not worthy to receive the food
of the gods I masturbated aye knowing full well there was nothing
left within me nary a drop of hope but lo the dawn did come instan-
taneously nonetheless and dispossessed me of my knowledge I gave
it away to kings, to kings thus I became: a patron to kings! [PULLS
KNIFE FROM BREAD] Now see me lance my flesh to teach you.
[CUTS INTO THE FLESH OF HIS FOREARM] Come here
come here come here one and two and three and with your fingers
search my wound now tell me be honest what do you think of it?

A wound is nothing said the third one. Whatever, that's the boring one. The extra one.

Give me a wound, father.

How now the froth the spangled milk pink the pink shroud when you wore it all the people in the cathedral were fated to die and they did die all died even your other the other the second one died and then you were grieving what? You were crying. I don't think so. You are crying. You are. Okay, fine. You are crying so you must go to hell what? You must go to hell. Hell. You know, hell. Hell the place behind the stars above the body no I can't find it.

The third one, the dull one is harbored by the priest. That's all he needs red wet houses boring because he likes it like that don't worry everyone likes it everyone likes it. But you Hey hey how now hey come on don't cry.

Don't cry you are above.

Above, you enter the scenery by chariot.

Your horses are kings with bits in their mouths. In your hands are the reins in your hands is the whip with which to scourgeth them. Go on, scourgeth them go on the kings the kings they are nothing.

Don't cry.

Don't cry you are above and you're fated, you are fated for another turn it's another try so go on get going go on to hell? Go! How? The stars! You must ask them. Stars, for example, I demand that you open your mouths and suck me forth, my body and my spirit please up up into the homicidal bowels of the clouds stars please vomit my limbs as ash into the air so that my spirit remains so my spirit alone ascends up up up into the kingdom of hell? Go!

Don't grieve.

You shall not lose you have not lost.

You haven't lost stop grieving go on.

Come on.

You have not lost come on.

You have not lost don't grieve.

You have not lost. You have not lost.

You have not lost. Come on.

You have not lost.

Don't grieve.

You have not lost.

Come on.

You have not lost.

You have not lost.

You have not lost.

You have not lost.

Come on.

You have not lost.

You have not lost.

You have not lost.

You have not lost.

You have not lost.

You have not lost.

Don't grieve.

Don't grieve.

Come on.

You have not lost.

You have not lost.

You have not lost.

You have not lost.

You have not lost.

You have not lost.

You have not lost.

You have not lost.

You have not lost.

You have not lost.

You have not lost.

You have not lost.

You have not lost.

You have not lost.

You have not lost.

You have not lost.

You have not lost.

You have not lost.

You have not lost.

You have not lost.

You have not lost.

You have not lost.

You have not lost.

You have not lost.

You have not lost.

You have not lost.

You have not lost.

You have not lost.

You have not lost.

You have not lost.

You have not lost.

You have not lost.

You have not lost.

You have not lost.

Don't grieve.

Come on.

Don't grieve.

Don't grieve.

You have not lost.

You have not lost.

You have not lost.

You have not lost.

You have not lost.

You have not lost.

You have not lost.

You have not lost.

You have not lost.

You have not lost.

You have not lost.

You have not lost.

You have not lost.

Come on.

Come on.

Come on.

You have not lost.

You have not lost.

You have not lost.

You have not lost.

You have not lost.

You have not lost.

You have not lost.

You have not lost.

You have not lost.

You have not lost.

You have not lost.

You have not lost.

You have not lost.

You have not lost.

You have not lost.

You have not lost.

You have not lost.

You have not lost.

You have not lost.

You have not lost.

You have not lost.

You have not lost.

You have not lost.

You have not lost.

You have not lost.

You have not lost.

You have not lost.

You have not lost.

You have not lost.

You have not lost.

You have not lost.

You have not lost.

You have not lost.

You have not lost.

You have not lost.

You have not lost.

You have not lost.

You have not lost.

You have not lost.

You have not lost.

You have not lost.

You have not lost.

You have not lost.

You have not lost.

You have not lost.

You have not lost.

You have not lost.

Come on.

Come on.

You have not lost.

You have not lost.

You have not lost.

You have not lost.

You have not lost.

You have not lost.

You have not lost.

You have not lost.

You have not lost.

You have not lost.

You have not lost.

You have not lost.

You have not lost.

You have not lost.

You have not lost.

You have not lost.

You have not lost.

You have not lost.

You have not lost.

You have not lost.

You have not lost.

You have not lost.

Come on.

You have not lost.

You have not lost.

You have not lost.

Come on.

You have not lost.

You have not lost.

III. DIALOGUE BETWEEN A PRIEST AND A DYING MAN

W ell, what I was trying to get at with that question was—

PRIEST: [...]

No, you're right. I must've hidden my intention. Well, I tried to signal it with the word labor. Maybe the signal failed? The question is an invitation to talk about the profession. The jobs awarded to my generation are not life-sustaining jobs.

PRIEST: [...]

Even my job. It's unsustainable. I'm always telling myself to go back on the market. To try to land something better. I'm operating under certain assumptions or wild fantasies about the structure of the profession, right? I could be telling myself the profession is no longer life sustaining. Go elsewhere.

PRIEST: [...]

Yes, I mean the money.

PRIEST: [...]

I'm talking about money, yeah.

PRIEST: [...]

Money, yes.

PRIEST: [...]

My salary is so low, I thought it was a typo. Then they slashed it to fix the budget. But yeah, time is also an issue for me, absolutely. You're right, I don't sleep. I think about driving to the city to find community, but then I think when? I'm working when I'm at work and when I'm at home. Teaching is ridiculous. My course load keeps increasing. I'm like This position, the one I'm working now, is not the position they offered me. And they're like This person, the person you are now, is not the person we hired. Are you telling us you don't want to work at a small, underfunded liberal-arts institution?

PRIEST: [...]

I don't know, I think one of the creepiest things you can say to a person is Tell me you don't want your job.

PRIEST: [...]

Yeah, next time I'll tell them they've got me all wrong. I'm the person who wants to work at a small, underfunded liberal-arts institution. Then I'll show them my university ID, so they can look upon the face of the person they hired.

PRIEST: [...]

Really? I want to work at a small, underfunded liberal-arts institution. Those words in that order have come out of somebody's mouth. In real life.

PRIEST: [...]

Though it goes without saying that this position was the only position offered to me, it also goes without saying that this position is the position that's most attractive to me... because the organization is small and underfunded. Before I actualized my desire to work for your fading organization, I dreamt of being a general type of human-styled person who wants to live by working in an endless sort of fashion at a small, underfunded liberal-arts institution in decline. You have no idea how much it excites me to know that when my time comes to an end on this fucked-to-death planet, I shall be granted the opportunity to apply to continue to manifest my dream of working for your organization in heaven, that perfected plane of infinite smallness and eternal scarcity—who said that? Who! When? Why? I don't believe it has ever come to pass. Still, I admit, if my wage were sustainable, or if my debt were forgiven, or even if there were some way to offer me discounted rent... maybe that's all it would take for me to believe I'm free to decide to endure whatever the—well, then I could decide to endure the job, right, if only to keep living my life.

PRIEST: [...]

But what I'm saying is there's no life to live, or there's no margin between living and working, due to the intensifying demands of the job that isn't paying me enough to build the life those intensifying demands are continuously eclipsing. So what the fuck am I doing?! Sometimes I try to calm myself with pipe dreams of leaving the profession, but then I think why? Nobody is going to pay me anything, not when they don't have to. There's a coercive aspect to this that makes me feel like I'm not in control. I'm always scared. I don't think I can handle this.

PRIEST: [...]

Well yeah, if I ever manage to leave—instead of, like, being forcibly removed—then everyone will assume I can't handle the lack of sleep, right? Or they'll say I left because, everything being equal, I just don't enjoy the work very much. Things are always equal to somebody with a marriage, a family, a career, a church, and real estate. Or maybe they'll tell each other, with smiles snaked on their faces, that I tricked myself into believing I'm better than the institution. Addled by hormones and specialness, I conned myself into believing that I deserve to live in excess of calculating survival by the lights of a shriveling horizon while twisting off dripping hunks of concern to chuck at students—because I'm one of those people who just doesn't care enough to know what it feels like to experience human sacrifice, durationally. But, like, the problem of materially ruining an entire generation of scholars and teachers will go unacknowledged. It's so fucked up.

PRIEST: [...]

Do I sound hyperbolic? I feel invisible and depressed.

PRIEST: [...]

I'm tenure track.

PRIEST: [...]

No, I am. I am tenure track.

PRIEST: [...]

Yeah, here also. Cost of living is outrageous.

PRIEST: [...]

Do you think there's a role for the university to play in securing something like housing for faculty?

PRIEST: [...]

Ah.

PRIEST: [...]

Okay.

PRIEST: [...]

Hmm.

PRIEST: [...]

I'm sure you do.

PRIEST: [...]

Are you serious? They start people at seventy-two thousand there?

A salary like that would be amazing for me. I can't imagine reaching that mark here.

PRIEST: […]

You seem to think I could strive for a situation like that.

PRIEST: […]

Okay, good. Because I want to.

PRIEST: […]

But I feel like a lot of these programs in creative writing, they want a name. I'm not a name. I'm not on social media. I don't do that.

PRIEST: […]

So what, are you saying maybe I should try? Would you recommend I try to make a name for myself? Oh god.

PRIEST: […]

Yeah, I know. That's why I'm sad. I don't doubt the value of what I'm doing. You don't have to tell me the work matters. Or that it matters when someone like me does it. I don't need that from you. My problem is I'm having trouble living a life. Everyone treats me as though I'm the keeper of the job, as though they've hired me to feed it. But it's supposed to be the other way around, right?

PRIEST: […]

I work, therefore I am. It's emotionally untenable. The terror. The atrophied relationships. I think turning thirty-five was a little moment for me. I thought Wow, I have a job. Finally. Yet I still refuse to imagine building friendships, intimacies, a home. I don't think I can. I don't think it's allowed. I kept thinking I'm going to wake up one day soon, like any day now, and the game will be over. I'll wake up and know that I've lost. That's when I decided to transition, which was brilliant because then there was a simple form of futurity at my disposal.

PRIEST: [...]

It seems unreal. I think that's because it is real. Next month, I'll have more hairs.

PRIEST: [...]

How did you manage when you were starting out? Did you just not sleep?

PRIEST: [...]

Here too. It's a very family-oriented, ritzy little suburb of a town. Even the gay people have spouses and kids, second incomes, mortgages, a church. I feel like the sickest animal. I'm that thing to avoid, like a raccoon in daylight or a pile of vomit. I haven't found a single interlocutor. Nobody at work will talk to me. Last August, at the first department meeting of the year, when everyone was gushing about landscaping projects and trips to the beach with kids, I had to work hard to not say anything. Because what could I share, ever? I had a glorious summer too, y'all. I grew hair on my thighs. It sure is great to be back at school with all you gummy-bear ghouls, and with hair on my thighs.

PRIEST: [...]

I should give yelling at myself a try. Look, you fucking pervert. You grew hair on your thighs. What more did you want out of life? I mean, come on. What you've managed to achieve? It's an immense, private delight. Congrats, asshole! Congrats.

PRIEST: [...]

I think I really believed transitioning would make me more palatable. So I'm an idiot.

PRIEST: [...]

I don't know. I think I still believe it. I feel like I've got to be more palatable now than I was in grad school. You know how I was. Wasn't it difficult to tolerate a person whose baseline was inchoate, reactive agony? Who wants to see something like that? I used to imagine that looking at me probably felt like being asked to do too much. Now I'm like Okay, all that stuff has been neutralized a bit. You're welcome.

PRIEST: [...]

Well, that's the thing. The agonized person is the person they hired. That's the one they wanted. It blows my mind.

PRIEST: [...]

One of them asked me if I know about a concept called structural oppression. He said one of the students just explained it to him. He sat me down and told me he thinks it's the system that's transphobic, not the individuals in the department.

PRIEST: [...]

I know. I know.

PRIEST: [...]

If I lost my job and my health care, I'd stand to lose access to my body. I'd stand to lose access to the life I'm trying to live before it started. For what? It's like everyone got flyswatters for Christmas this year, and they can't wait to fucking use them.

PRIEST: [...]

Never punch up. That's the only rule in the academy. It's the only rule that matters. It's the only rule anyone seems to follow. That means the legitimate harms incurred in this space will never be made right. Whatever operating system people are using to run their psychologies, it's set up to continuously sublimate desires for justice and restoration into endless projects of scapegoating and punching down—and all of it in the name of professionalism.

PRIEST: [...]

After everything that's happened, I cannot imagine allowing myself to feel threatened or even merely annoyed by anybody on a lower rung. No amount of coercion could get me to turn on a person in need. They couldn't bribe me to swat at a fly. I don't care if it's buzzing or biting. I don't care what pathogens it carries on its tongue. I don't care if it undermines the university as an institution. I will not be moved to squash it. That's not what violence is for. It's such a waste. It's such a fucking waste. I'm trying to grow up so I can die like a normal person, but if they really want to take that away from me—fine. Fine. Boil me alive. I'll go out like Barabas. I will curse to the best of my vocabulary until I lose consciousness.

PRIEST: [...]

Thanks.

PRIEST: [...]

Thank you.

PRIEST: [...]

Thank you.

PRIEST: [...]

Thank you, seriously. Yeah, I'll try the market again. So yes, I'll appreciate your support. Of course. Thank you. And I'll be in touch. I will.

PRIEST: [...]

Thanks.

PRIEST: [...]

Sure, yes. Honestly, this interview has turned out better than I imagined it would. I don't really get to have conversations like this. You've really—

PRIEST: [...]

I never get the opportunity. Never. I know this has been a thousand times more meaningful for me. Really, thank you for talking with me.

PRIEST: [...]

Okay.

PRIEST: [...]

Okay. Yes.

PRIEST: [...]

Mmhmm.

PRIEST: [...]

Mmhmm. You too.

PRIEST: [...]

You too.

PRIEST: [...]

Well, thank you.

PRIEST: [...]

Thank you.

PRIEST: [...]

It does. It means so much to me. It means so much that you're even acknowledging what I'm saying. With some mentors there'd just be disavowal, but you've been—

PRIEST: [...]

You've—

PRIEST: [...]

Yeah?

PRIEST: [...]

I know. Sometimes I'm able to access a gross store of knowledge from deep within myself. Like, if I were ever offered that R1 job? I know I'd be so tempted to take it, repress all this pain, and enjoy the rest of my life. But Jesus Christ. What the fuck. Nobody should do a thing like that.

IV. THE USE OF PLEASURE

WHAT IS THE CAUSE OF MY ILLUSION of seeing a spirit in the triangle of art? Philosophy has nothing to say; science can only suspend judgement, pending a proper and methodical investigation.

MARQUIS DE SADE presents a purely materialistic, rational statement when he writes, "Pricks, aye, pricks, those are my gods, those are my kin, my boon companions, unto me they are everything, I live in the name of nothing but the penis sublime; and when it is not in my cunt, nor in my ass, it is so firmly anchored in my thoughts that the day they dissect me it will be found in my brain." All sense impressions are dependent upon changes in the brain, and so it follows that the phenomenal universe is the creation of the ego.

THE SERPENT IS COILED in the space between the outer and inner circles, and it is bright deep yellow. The square in the center of the circle, where the word "Master" is written, is filled in with red. The triangle is to be made two feet distant from the circle. The video call is transcribed in the space between the circle and the triangle, which is green.

RAY:

Hi, thanks for speaking with me! I know how carefully you guard your image, so I just want to reiterate how grateful I am that you've agreed to do the interview. I'm so happy, you have no idea. [LAUGH-TER]

RACHILDE:

All right. You're welcome. I'll have to keep my camera off. I hope you don't mind. The connection is frayed. Can you hear me?

RAY:

You sound frayed. [LAUGHTER] Scratchy.

RACHILDE:

Can you understand me?

RAY

Yes, but there's some distortion. I think what I'm hearing isn't your actual voice. Not that I need to hear it—I don't—that would be a weird thing to need. [LAUGHTER] [BLUSHING] Sorry, I'm trying to say I don't need it because I respect your privacy.

RACHILDE:

You're okay.

RAY:

Okay thanks.

RACHILDE:	You followed my instructions.
RAY:	Well yeah.
RACHILDE:	Yeah.
RAY:	Yes and no. [LAUGHTER] I don't come from a religious background, so I had to improvise. Honestly, I didn't even know there were seven gods. [LAUGHTER] I thought there was just one because, like, that's the whole point. Or that's the brand, you know? [LAUGHTER]
RACHILDE:	There are seven names for the Divine.
RAY:	Right, well I didn't know the names. But I read your emails a bunch of times— they're so amazing—and the sense I got was this is one of those situations where an obedience to form matters more than a respect for content. I guess I figured I could sub in my own names. Invoke, like, a personal pantheon or something, you know? [LAUGHTER]
RACHILDE:	Okay. The problem has a source.
RAY:	The problem?
RACHILDE:	Our weak connection.
RAY:	Our weak connection! That's really sad.

[LAUGHTER] Do you want to log out and try again? Sometimes that's a fix. Or is it a myth? You know, like blowing on the cartridge. Do you remember doing that? Blowing on the cartridge? [LAUGHTER] Sorry, I have no idea if you're my age. [LAUGHTER]

RACHILDE: Into the cartridge. You did follow the in-structions.

RAY: Yeah.

RACHILDE: Aroused the coiled splendor within you?

RAY: That is a description of my feelings, yes. [LAUGHTER]

RACHILDE: I mean is it according to your will that we are speaking?

RAY: Oh god: absolutely! [LAUGHTER] Thank you for obliging me. To be clear, I've want-ed this conversation to happen for such a long time. Seriously, I'm so happy. The coil is aroused.

RACHILDE: It's fine then. Everything will be okay.

RAY: Okay. Really?

RACHILDE: Yes. This isn't science.

RAY: Right. I don't think it's science. I just can't tell if—I don't know what this is. [LAUGH-TER] I thought your emails were meant to be funny, you know? Like in a serious way? Or I assumed we were playing? I also thought He's fucking with me. I still think that's what's happening. I wish I could see your expression. [LAUGHTER] Sorry. Honestly, um, whatever this is, I'm into it. I watch a lot of Kenneth Anger, so. I inscribed his name. [LAUGHTER]

RACHILDE: Kenneth Anger's name.

RAY: On the serpent, yeah. Marlowe's, too. I want to be the Jew of Malta! [LAUGHTER] Also, Marquis de Sade. I read somewhere, I think it was in *BOMB*, that you've also been influenced by Sade. We could begin the interview there. Would you want to tell me about your relationship to Sade and how his work has shaped your approach to filmmaking?

RACHILDE: You inscribed Sade's name.

RAY: Yeah. Of course. [LAUGHTER]

RACHILDE: He is dead.

RAY: [LAUGHTER] I know.

RACHILDE: You know.

RAY: Well. Yeah.

RACHILDE: Spirit is alive.

RAY: Is it? [LAUGHTER] Doesn't feel that way.

RACHILDE: Gods are living, always.

RAY: Okay. What I'm saying is some of mine died. Well, but Culture Club got back together, I think. Does that count? They reincarnated. [LAUGHTER] Or no, reanimated? Resurrected! They resurrected, yeah. [LAUGHTER]

RACHILDE: [GROWLING] This is the source.

RAY: [BLUSHING] Of our weak connection.

RACHILDE: Yes.

RAY: [BLUSHING] I'm sorry. Now I think you're being serious. Hey, do you want to log off really quick? We could start the call again and see if that helps. Or listen, would you prefer to reschedule?

RACHILDE: You can hear me? You understand me.

RAY: Yeah. Yes.

RACHILDE: Okay then. Nothing is wrong.

RAY:	Okay, thank god. How are you? [LAUGH-TER]
RACHILDE:	Buoyed. I was psyched to receive your email.
RAY:	[LAUGHTER]
RACHILDE:	I am psyched.
RAY:	I don't know. If you're psyched, then I'm ecstatic. [LAUGHTER] I wasn't expecting a reply. It's been three years. [LAUGHTER]
RACHILDE:	I apologize. Time is odd.
RAY:	Sure, sure. [LAUGHTER] Well, that's okay. That's okay. [LAUGHTER] Sorry. I'm sorry I'm laughing so much. [LAUGH-TER] I'm just really happy, seriously. [LAUGHTER]
RACHILDE:	Me too. I'm all pleasure and purple.
RAY:	Oh, okay. [LAUGHTER] Well, your films meant so much to me when I was a graduate student. I just watched *The Strange Case* again this morning because I wrote about it in my shitty dissertation, which I'm currently trying to revise into something, I don't know, whatever, less shitty? [LAUGHTER] Maybe we should begin the interview there. Do you want to talk about *The Strange Case*?

RACHILDE: Okay. Sure.

RAY: Excellent. This is awesome. [LAUGHTER]
                 You launched your career by publishing a
                 series of sadistic montages on YouTube un-
                 der the channel name Rachilde. For read-
                 ers who may be unaware, the pseudonym
                 is an homage to the nineteenth-century
                 decadent novelist of the same name—

RACHILDE: And the ghost of the nobleman residing
                 in the novelist's body, also called Rachilde.
                 One of my favorite writers.

RAY: Right, okay. The cinematography of *The
                 Strange Case* marks a departure from the
                 remediated quality of your earlier works.
                 Not only is *The Strange Case* your first at-
                 tempt at telling an original story with a co-
                 herent linear narrative, it's also your feature
                 debut. And it's basically a satiric documen-
                 tary, correct? A mockumentary?

RACHILDE: More or less.

RAY: A note to readers who have yet to view *The
                 Strange Case*: it is possible to stream the
                 film for free at https://www.youtube.com/
                 watch?v=rSZw_EWojEY.

RACHILDE: It is possible. Which is not to say it is worth
                 your while.

RAY: Oh stop! *The Strange Case* is a fantas-
tic movie! It's a satire of academia in pres-
ent-day America. The film's principal characters are comp-lit professors employed in
tenured positions at East Coast research
institutions. They appear to be white and
pushing sixty years of age. They are not
queer, not explicitly. However, like decay-
ing European aristocrats, they're straight in
a way that's a little bit gay. [BLUSHING]
Sorry, I'm not sure how else to put it. Then
there's the undeniable homosocial eroticism structuring the relationships in the
group, of course, which, you know, always
reads as violently repressed homosexual
desire [BLUSHING] to me. Okay so *The
Strange Case* chronicles these characters
and their relationships with one another as
they collaborate to deliver a panel presentation before a small audience of like-minded
academics at a humanities center in NYC.
The subject of the presentation is the Yale
school of deconstruction. What begins as
a grotesque memorial to deconstruction at
Yale, quickly burgeons into something like
a hysterical funeral service for post-struc-
turalism writ large. Lots of crying and raging, lots of tripping the wire separating wet
nostalgia for the '80s from irate bitterness
because it is no longer the '80s. Somehow

the energy is both farcical and dangerous. Spoiler: there's a moment near the end when the malevolent ghost of Paul de Man takes possession of the body of one of the panelists! [LAUGHTER] I want to ask you about the decisions you made when you were casting the film. I could be wrong, but my understanding is that you declined to use professional actors, opting instead to contract working academics who play versions of themselves on the screen. What did it take to convince these academics to appear as themselves? Was it an explicit goal of yours to humiliate these people and their life's work? If so, how did you square that objective with the political and ethical commitments of your creative project as a whole?

RACHILDE: The actors were willing to humiliate themselves. Post-structuralists are masochists of the most adolescently authoritarian variety. Crying and raging is their métier. Yes, those academics had quite a bit of fun acting in my movie—and wouldn't you know, they were unchanged by the experience. The process effected zero transformation upon the structuring logic of their relationships. Their sociality remained catatonically static. To the individual panelists, however, there came moderate increases in wealth and power, which made me want to kill myself, so I did. For those reasons and others, I consider *The Strange Case* to be a cosmic failure. Nobody likes *The Strange Case*, by the way. You're the only person I've found who seems to be genuinely taken with the film. Most viewers feel nothing, except for the vaguest longing to recuperate a portion of the pure unadulterated life that is quietly extracted as the parcel of time one forfeits in watching it. They do not care for or cannot detect the film's irony. They see the flat, insipid image of a violently repressed academic delivering a dreary presentation on a dated subject that is at best of no consequence and at worst a virulent distraction from everything that matters.

RAY:

I'm sorry. I guess all I can do is underscore my gratitude. As I told you in my email, it felt like a miracle to find *The Strange Case* precisely when I needed it most. The department that educated me was enthralled by deconstruction, and I rejected it. I was not a good student. Well, no. It's more like I refused to submit to the law. No. I don't know. Nothing I've said is accurate. It isn't meaningful, the difference between refusal and failure. I can remember everything I did. But I'm unable to access the truth of my actions.

RACHILDE:	The truth of action is the force of the will.
RAY:	In the end, I decided to let them believe they had ascertained through the augury of the exam that I just didn't know how to read. Then, instantaneously appeased by the con, they awarded me the degree, which I traded for the seeds that I swallow to engender the breath of the demon I'm becoming.
RACHILDE:	Listen, the world is not diminished by the inch each time you achieve the alignment of body and will; it is multiplied. Your only task is to learn the infinite ways there are for relishing it: the surplus of pleasure and knowledge brought on by the marvelous alignment. Are you willing to learn?
RAY:	I'm not a student anymore.
RACHILDE:	That's okay. Are you willing?
RAY:	Everything's just families and houses now. Without time, without art. Nobody to write, no writing. There's a job and the conversation about liking it. How is that even possible?
RACHILDE:	I don't know. It's possible.
RAY:	What the fuck. Now it's just curdling.

Curdling and talking about liking it. I mean,
come on, what is that? A parasitical passion
for excommunicating thought. I swear it's a
passion, the liking. It perfects them by re-
placing them with itself. Dumb aspics, they
suck it in like jellied air. They donate themselves to it, some thicker apocalypse stron-
ger than nature. Why? For what? Oh my
god, fuck their families. Fuck their houses.
I won't curdle. I will not congeal. Fuck that.
I'll die. Yeah, I guess I'll just die.

RACHILDE: No.

RAY: But they've left me for dead.

RACHILDE: You're not dead.

RAY: Those fuckers. Those congealing fuckers.
              They'll just watch.

RACHILDE: All right.

RAY: I'm exaggerating, sure.

RACHILDE: You resent them.

RAY: I horrify them.

RACHILDE: The horror is senseless. It means nothing.

RAY: It's tucked up in the fold of their liking. The
              seam of my resentment.

RACHILDE:	They've bet on the loss. Don't bet on the loss.
RAY:	Blackish jelly. The black currant emptied of time. Nothing comes after. You think I am free to leave. No, I am used.
RACHILDE:	But there are finer uses. There are finer ways to get used. Our exquisite collaboration. Come now. [BARKING] You're an artist. You're a writer, are you not? Let's begin.
RAY:	Who are you?
RACHILDE:	Your collaborator.
RAY:	I saw you. In the woods?
RACHILDE:	[SNORTING] [PUFFING]
RAY:	What? Oh my god. Fuck you.
RACHILDE:	[GROWLING]
RAY:	But I wanted to talk to you! I tried to feed you that carrot. Jesus Christ, that fucking baby carrot! You trotted off. You just trotted away, like some kind of trotting animal in the woods—and then the world clicked shut. I didn't even know what to call you, you asshole! I searched for weeks. I looked for you, don't you know, with those fucking baby carrots in my pockets like some kind of mad—oh my god, they believe I am mad.

RACHILDE: Are you not mad?

RAY: I'm livid. [GROWLING] Livid, before
              them: strangers! They're strangers, oh my
              god. But come on, who serves baby carrots?
              I mean fuck god, fuck. Must everything be
              meager and weak? Has austerity come for
              the vegetables, too? Nothing is plentiful
              but sorrow and shame, nothing gigantic
              but exhaustion? And what, I'm just sup-
              posed to swallow it? A baby carrot. Really?
              Some people eat with their eyes, you know!
              I mean fuck, the least they could've done is
              given me something to want! A standard
              carrot at the very least. Have you ever seen
              one? A standard carrot? It's a glorious veg-
              etable! Put a standard carrot next to a baby
              carrot atop one of those fucked rustic
              boards they use to arrange their food on
              and there's no contest. I pity the baby car-
              rot. And I didn't even want to have dinner!
              Don't you know that? That's the thing. I
              had wanted to set up a meeting, to do it
              professionally. They were the ones who
              suggested we have dinner. Really? Okay,
              but now? And sure, the house was nice.
              Also, they handed me a bunch of beers, like
              one after another, which I downed pretty
              rapidly—to be philanthropic, mind you! I
              can't admire a house whilst sober. There

can't be many people on this earth with the ability to achieve something like that! You have to do that, you know. You have to say it aloud. Nice house. Stunning, absolutely stunning. I mean that kind of shit? It doesn't come easily. Plus I was starving so I didn't want to overdo it, the enthusiasm, or else the tour would never end! But that's not the point. The point is dinner was baby carrots. *Just* baby carrots. A hill of them. A small hill. A hillock? A pile on a wooden cutting board. Because that's what it was. It's what those things are! Average, run-of-the-mill cutting boards. Drape the foods just so and you've got yourself a mood. No, you don't. You don't. Not if you're serving carrots. *Just* carrots. Babies! Plus they dropped it. The cutting board. They didn't even lower it gently. They did not set it down hospitably. They dropped it from a great height. I mean come on. Carrots rolling all over the place. That's not dinner, it's a crudité. For a pony! Also a mindfuck, right? I swear it was some half-baked attempt to throw me off my game. So I decided to launch into it, my whole spiel. Thanks but no thanks, I'm gonna politely bow out now. You know what I mean. I'm gonna delicately extricate myself from this, this project? I almost said cult! But I didn't think they'd take kindly to that word. So okay, this project, it's been fairly meaningful, yeah? It was very slightly meaningful while it lasted, sure. At least we got dinner out of it, am I right? How nice are these carrots? And the house? And the cutting board? Stunning, stunning specimens of American carpentry. So congrats, okay? Congrats and goodbye. Well, I don't think they were ready to hear something like that. Or maybe they were ready to hear it, that's the thing, because they were prepared. They had prepared. They'd printed it out and everything, the paperwork. Slapped it down, that infernal packet, right next to the cutting board and the carrots. Would I mind filling it out? It might persuade me to change my mind. It's a game changer, this paperwork. Isn't that what I want? What I long for? A change? They'd needed one too. Because they'd been suicidal. Frankly, they whispered. They were frankly and literally suicidal. But then they completed the paperwork. Next, they submitted the paperwork. Promptly, the paperwork was honored, and the loan was deposited into the account. See for yourself. This is a house, is it not? It is, I said. Congrats? And they said Thank you. Yep, they said, we think we are happy now. You heard me. They said they think they are happy now. They think? And then they said Right? Like to one another. And they said it again. They exchanged rights with one another. Right? Right. Right? Right. Right? Right? Right? Right? Then I asked them to stop because when you say it that way it isn't very convincing. I wasn't convinced. Plus, I didn't want a house. I wanted—oh, fuck it. I didn't know how to put it to them. Oh my god. Whatever. I wanted a collaborator. You know. I wanted a collaborator. All right, they said. Just don't do anything rash, not before checking out the art department. I told them I already did that. I checked it out. You checked it out, they said. And? There's nobody. Nobody, nothing, nada, et cetera. Really, they said. There's nobody who shaves the sides of their head? So then I was like What the fuck you know that's not what I mean! I mean sure hair matters a little. At a certain stage or a particular hour of the day, it matters a little; to be honest theirs was beginning to become a tiny problem for me. But first of all, what they said is not an accurate description of my hair! Secondly, hair is last on my list, okay? Last! Hair is fairly beside the point, wouldn't you agree? They crossed their arms. We think our hair is

fairly alternative, they said. Fairly alternative? Yes, they said. Fairly alternative. Alternative, unconventional, nonconform-
ing... you get it, take your pick. I don't
want it, I said. Because it's hair. It's your
hair, I said. Your hair. What do you expect
me to do with it? Would you like me to eat
it? Do you want me to eat your hair? What,
I suppose I should chop it up and make a
savory paste with it? Dip those baby carrots into it and swallow it? Then what, I
shall live here in your ghastly forever like I
don't know some kind of petrified gum-
drop? Fine! I can do that. I'll eat your hair,
all right? I'll eat it straight off your gelati-
nous heads if that's what you need. I want
to survive the evening. I want to leave this
house alive. Do you hear? NO ONE
TOUCHES ME. I DON'T GET HURT.
They took a step back and told me to calm
down. Hey now, they said. Hey now, hey.
All we're saying is our hair is fairly nonnormative so we're, like, you know, basically
friendly. Oh my god! Don't say that! Never
say that! Before they'd said that, I was beginning to suspect the commentary on hair
was merely a diabolical tool devised by
them to disavow what I—you know what I
mean—a simpleton's gambit, constructed
in their image, to completely efface and

absolutely deny my—perhaps they only wanted some congrats? Congrats on the hair. Congrats on the cutting board. Congrats on the house. Thank you, they said. They said Yep, we think our life here is fairly nice. You heard me. They told me they think their life is nice. Then they said Right a bunch of times while flipping open the packet of papers and pressing a pen into the palm of my hand. That's when I snapped—I'm speaking literally now—the pen in two. Recently I've become fairly strong. Physically strong, basically. Not emotionally strong. Not socially strong. Which probably explains why I did what I did. I grabbed two handfuls of baby carrots and fled into the woods. Oh, they've got some woods behind their house all right. It really was a stunning situation, that whole apparatus. I'd been dreaming about fleeing into those woods, but I was hungry so I stuffed some baby carrots into the pockets of my jeans before exiting through the backdoor. The house came with a back door, yep. Stunning! Congrats! I sprinted through the back door, maybe breaking it? Look, this was a fragile apparatus. The whole situation, it was fragile as fuck—and I had become fairly strong, physically. I tore through the back door maybe literally, though I didn't feel any pain, and I promptly slipped into the woods. Immediately, I spotted you, which was miraculous, totally miraculous—fuck the art department—and I had all those baby carrots on me, remember? I was pretty sure you ate those. Carrots are a portion of your diet, correct? What I mean is I figured your head probably ate them. Because I noticed, beholding you fleetingly in the woods, that you're a composite. You're a little bit of a composite, okay? That's fine, I don't mind. I'm merely trying to explain my behavior. I was operating under the assumption that carrots are standard fare for the type of head you have. Therefore, I extended a carrot to you as an offering. You ran away, I gave chase, and then they located me. They dragged me back to their house (Congrats!) and yanked me indoors. It made them worry intensively, they said, to watch me run off like that into their woods. And then to find me just running like that? In their woods? They hope it wasn't due to anything they had said. They meant no offense by whatever it was. Okay, I said. And the paperwork? The paperwork, they said. Don't be silly. Don't give that paperwork another thought, not tonight. We'll try again tomorrow. Because one would be wise to sign the papers first thing in the morning. But for now, one should rest. Like right here and at once. Well I flipped out. They couldn't possibly believe that I was psychologically prepared to spend the night in their house with them. Thanks but no thanks, I said. I'll sleep in the woods. The bleeding moon is oozing and brighter than advertised, and I want to lie beneath it to catch the drippings in my throat. I mean have you ever had such an epiphany? Sprinted into the woods and changed your entire point of view vis-à-vis your career? I gushed for a while about the experience, which they tolerated, but they weren't paying attention. They didn't get what I was trying to say. I wasn't saying a man or a deer. I wasn't saying a man and a deer. I wasn't even saying a man plus a deer. Throw those words away, okay? Listen. What I'm saying is a deer with a masculine chest. I'm saying I saw a deer with a masculine chest. In your woods! I saw a deer with a masculine chest in your woods. Do you hear? Yes, they said, gross. Then what they did next was they made a noise like eek and shut me inside one of the smaller rooms. They told me to collect myself. I was like Jesus Christ what the fuck is this? Turns out they were standing on the other side of the door, so they replied. It's a house. I told them congrats on the house and then I broke out of it, slipping into the woods once more. Again, they grabbed me and dragged me. This time to the station wagon. They yanked me straight up inside of it. Very nice, a hatchback. Basically, they loaded me up and drove me home. Deposited me on the lawn of the apartment complex. I returned to them on foot, pretty much immediately. I jogged right over. Into the woods. I kept doing that. Roaming their property, mad creep with baby carrots—and it hardly matters the identities of the twisted minds or fairly nonnormative hairs that did once conspire to serve that diminutive, demonic dinner. Because now the carrots are mine. They are mine now, mine. My cross. Fucking baby cross! That's a pathetic way to make a name for oneself. Wouldn't you agree?

RACHILDE: All right. There, there. I'll agree, sure. I'm agreeing with you, see? Everything will be okay. But you must tell me. Tell me honestly. Did you eat it?

RAY: What. The hair?

RACHILDE: Be honest with me. Did you eat any portion at all? Any fraction, no matter how small or short?

RAY:	Did I eat it. Fuck you! I wouldn't handle it with falconer's gloves! I wouldn't poke its bloated remains with—
RACHILDE:	Good! You did good, okay? Our future lives. ☺Look, I don't want to waste any more time on this matter. It sounds like you had an abominable dinner. That dinner was a hazard, okay? A legitimate trauma. We've all had them. Come, come. You'll be all right. This is me comforting you from an impossible distance, which I suggest we close, officially. Now, as I touched upon earlier in our conversation, I did something very stupid in 2017. I killed myself. Yet the desire to finish my work remains. I want to finish my work. I need to finish my work. You're an artist, a writer. You understand.
RAY:	Sure. Of course.
RACHILDE:	Excellent, very well. For transparency's sake, please allow me to explain that even though natural law will automatically prohibit something like a refusal between us to occur, I have decided nonetheless to pitch my proposition as a promise because I suspect the words will move you more powerfully in that form given the experiences you've shared with me. That dinner was truly unconscionable.

RAY: It was vile. Right?

RACHILDE: You are in need. You yearn for a promise.
                Please, allow me to give one to you. If you
                should consent to accept me into your con-
                tainer, which is becoming gigantic and will
                only grow in marvelous dimension as our
                days unfold, then I will eat the baby carrot.
                We shall consume the miniature vegetable
                together. You have my word. I will never re-
                fuse you again.

RAY: Thank you. I don't know what to say.

RACHILDE: I require consent. You must say yes.

RAY: I feel I should tell you I hate baby carrots.

RACHILDE: The fact of their existence justifies the no-
                tion of genocide.

RAY: Wow. [LAUGHTER] I guess I'm not that
                extreme. I mean, I certainly understand
                baby carrots. I get them, okay? They're
                the same as standard carrots. You think I
                don't know that? It's literally the same ma-
                terial, just shaped differently or cut in a
                different fashion. I know, but I don't care.
                Because I don't enjoy them. I don't know
                why. [BLUSHING] The babies taste like
                shit to me.

RACHILDE: [SHOUTING IN LATIN] A pox on the house of baby carrots!

RAY: Exactly, exactly. [LAUGHTER] Okay so what I enjoy is basically writing all day. I mean, whenever a day exists. Frequently reading. Then, in the evening, I like to put on headphones, step outside, and listen to music—it must be loud—whilst sucking a beer or a cigarette.

RACHILDE: Fine.

RAY: And what, you're suggesting we'd be doing that together? Like, encased in the body, the air, and time?

RACHILDE: That is my promise to you.

RAY: Oh my god, I knew it. I fucking knew it. I knew there was more. Another step or stage, a greater form of enormity. I've been waiting for it. You know?

RACHILDE: I do. But you must say it. [GROWLING] Say yes.

RAY: Yes.

TO MAKE THE GREATER CURSE, observe thou also the moon in thy working, for

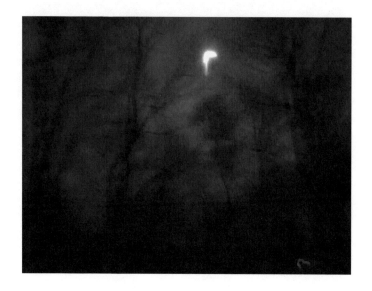

NOTES & ACKNOWLEDGMENTS

Many components used in the collage tableaus were sourced from photos I captured by pointing a toy camera at my television while it was playing Kenneth Anger's *Inauguration of the Pleasure Dome* and James Whale's *Bride of Frankenstein*; and while it was streaming YouTube clips of lectures and interviews featuring Georges Bataille, Jacques Derrida, and Jacques Lacan.

The sections called "Dialogue Between a Priest and a Dying Man" reimagine Marquis de Sade's dialogue of the same name.

The illustration of Furfur directly following the "Dear Committee" chapter was created by Louis Le Breton for the 1863 edition of Jacques Collin de Plancy's *Dictionnaire Infernal*.

"Autobiographical Animal" responds to and reinterprets Jacques

Derrida's ten-hour address to the 1997 Cérisy conference, titled "The Autobiographical Animal" (published as *The Animal That Therefore I Am*, trans. David Wills). It's also informed by Edgar Allan Poe's "The Tell-Tale Heart." This piece first appeared in *ANMLY*.

"Seminar XXXXXXIVX: Rats in the Maze at the School of Love" borrows and mashes up bits of language from Jacques Lacan's "God and the Jouissance of ~~The~~ Woman" (trans. Jacqueline Rose) and "The Rat in the Maze" (trans. Bruce Fink), and Jacques Derrida's "The Double Session" (trans. Barbara Johnson). The diptych directly following this chapter is captioned by a line lifted from *Bride of Frankenstein*.

"Severin" responds to and reinterprets *Venus in Furs* by Leopold von Sacher-Masoch. This piece first appeared in *The Account*.

"Sacrament" reinterprets and explicates plot elements in *A Sentimental Journey Through France and Italy* by Laurence Sterne. The image directly following this chapter is lifted from *Infant Chimpanzee and Human Child* by N.N. Ladygina-Kohts; it is captioned by a phrase borrowed from Jacques Derrida's "The Double Session" (trans. Barbara Johnson). This piece first appeared in *DIAGRAM*.

Small portions of "You Hated Yourself" borrow and remix phrases from essays, letters, and interviews by Jacques Derrida, Georges Bataille, and Alain Robbe-Grillet. This piece first appeared in *Western Humanities Review*.

"The Strange Case of the Yale School: How to Review a Movie" reinterprets and borrows transcribed dialogue from a scholarly presentation on the Yale school of deconstruction, hosted by the NYU Center for the Humanities and uploaded to YouTube in 2016. The six "flipping my fingers" images that directly follow the chapter were created by pointing a toy camera at my television while it was streaming the presentation.

Small portions of "The Host" appropriate lines and plot points from Christopher Marlowe's *Doctor Faustus* and *Tamburlaine The Great, Parts I & II*. This piece first appeared in *Black Warrior Review*.

"The Use of Pleasure" appropriates a small number of passages from Marquis de Sade's *Juliet* (trans. Austryn Wainhouse) and Aleister Crowley's *The Goetia: The Lesser Key of Solomon the King*. It also rewrites and incorporates a small number of phrases from *Poems of Paul Celan* by Paul Celan (trans. Michael Hamburger). It lifts its title from Michel Foucault's *The History of Sexuality, Vol. 2*; and it's haunted by Rachilde's *Monsieur Vénus*, S. Ansky's *The Dybbuk*, and Marcin Wrona's *Demon*. I captured the image at the end with my phone in Fredericksburg, Virginia. This piece first appeared in *Territory*.

I would like to express my gratitude to the editors of the aforementioned journals for publishing and championing portions of this project. Thank you, Sarah Clark. I thank everyone at FC2 and the University of Alabama Press for publishing my book. Thank you, Sarah Blackman, Jon Berry, Brian Conn, Steve Halle, Michael Mejia, Marream Krollos, Vi Khi Nao, Aimee Parkison, Hilary Plum, Lou Robinson, Joanna Ruocco, Blanche Sarratt, and Daniel Waterman. I'd like to thank the English Department at Michigan State University, the English Department at the University of Utah, and the NEA Literature Fellowships program for funding and time. I want to thank Mary Wash Creative Writing and Trans Lit students. I will thank my colleagues: Laura Bylenok, Chris Foss, Jonathan Levin, Colin Rafferty, and Warren Rochelle. Thank you, Danny Tweedy, Craig Vasey, and Laura Wilson. I want to express my gratitude to the Gay Reads group and to the mentors and friends who were there while the writing was happening. Thank you, Israel Aguilar Pacheco, Jessica Alexander, Lindsey Appell, Evie Atom Atkinson, Caren Beilin, Scott Black, Nora Bonner, Grace Cameron, PJ Carlisle, Jean-Paul Cauvin, Rhett Cooper, Jeffrey Deshell, Lily Duffy, Jim Gardner, Jose de la Garza Valenzuela, Molly Gaudry, Sloane Holzer, Ellie Hutcherson, Andrew Lee, Antony Lin, Jenny Marion, Jolie Maya-Altschuler, E.L. McCallum, Ronika McClain, Paula Mendoza, Joseph Metz, Andi Olsen, Lance Olsen, Steve Owen, Richard Preiss, James Pryor, Joe Sacksteder, Katie Jean Shinkle, Maeera Shreiber, Robin Silbergleid, Ryan Skrabalak, Evan Steuber, Kathryn Bond Stockton, Melanie Rae Thon, Ed Trefts, Divya Victor, and Mir Yarfitz.